The Last Hurrah

A PHOEBE KORNEAL MYSTERY SERIES

BOOK 1

The Last Hurrah

A Phoebe Korneal Mystery

GaGa Gabardi & Judilee Butler

The Last Hurrah

PHOEBE KORNEAL MYSTERY SERIES
BOOK 1

FIRST EDITION

This story is dedicated to the ones we love.

CONTENTS

INTRODUCTION

At over 10,000 feet in altitude, our fictional setting is in Oresville, Green County, Colorado, with a population of approximately 2,000. The citizens of Oresville thrive in 2015 with a foothold in the mining spirit of the mid-1800s. Although several of our characters have moved to Oresville from other states, they feel the acceptance and camaraderie of our characters who were born and raised in this high mountain town.

Our main character, Deputy Sheriff and occasional detective, Phoebe Korneal, is a strong, independent woman, much like the historical women of Oresville who moved with or followed their families to settle the west, enduring hardshi and struggles never anticipated in their *civilized lives* in the eastern United States.

Gold prospecting has always been and still is an interesting hobby in the central mountains of Colorado. In our stor, the demise of Old Al Lewis, a lifetime prospector, is a curious event for someone as healthy as he appeared to be. Phobe must work to solve the puzzle of Old Al's death. Her sidkick, Carrie Jean, will happily share the news in her daily E3last! for the local newspaper.

This is the beauty of the small town of Oresville, Colorao. Anything that happens makes a difference to the whole twn and its residents. The local newspaper reports everything and anything in the tradition of the role of newspaers in settling the western territories. Newspapers in the 800s were part and parcel to the importance of community in mountain towns and today remain an integral part of ll small-town communities.

Referencing the Colorado National Mining Hall of Fame and Museum helped us understand much about the area we were writing about in this fun story. The museum does a great job of documenting the history and challenges of life in the 1800s, as well as the many strong-minded and adventurous people attracted to mining. The history of the area supports the continuing independent culture of the state.

Colorado became the Centennial State in 1876, one hundred years after the signing of the Declaration of Independence. Today, Colorado is a state with residents

2

who maintain this collective, independent culture of self-esteem, appreciation for the environment, and value of historical preservation. This is the perspective we bring to Oresville and our characters.

Join Phoebe and her crew of interesting and somewhat eccentric fellow Oresvillians to unravel the mystery of Old Al's sudden demise. As autumn approaches in Oresville, and a cold wind begins to blow, this light murder mystery will keep you warm at night. Read on!

THE CRIME

G ood Morning, we're having a great day at the Green County Sheriff's Office. Rosalind Marie Boudreaux speaking."

"Roz, I need to speak with the sheriff now."

"Who's calling, please?" The standard question for their recorded line.

"Roz, you know this is Augusta, and I need to talk with Joe right now."

"What's the problem now, Augusta?"

"I'm at the abandoned Sunshine mine, and Al is dead."

"C'mon, Augusta. I thought we were done with this nonsense, and y'all didn't even bother to marry this one."

Roz and Augusta had been friends, or at least friendly, since Roz came to Oresville, and she felt comfortable giving Augusta a hard time. Even by Roz's standards, Augusta's five marriages seemed a bit much.

"Don't let's talk about the past now, Roz. Didn't you hear me? Al is dead! I'm sitting at the Sunshine looking at the body of good ol' Al. I'm not up for a chat. I just need Joe to get on out here. Is he there, or is he still at the Buns Up Bakery?"

"Geez Augusta, y'all know he really doesn't open for business until about ten-ish. He doesn't take kindly to interruptin' his mornin' campaignin'. But, a death? Maybe I should call him. Hold on a minute."

Switching to the other phone line, Roz called the sheriff's cell phone. "Hey Joe, I've got Augusta on hold on the other line. She's up at the Sunshine. She found Old Al dead there. Sorry to cut your politicking pastry time short, but I think she needs you up there ASAP."

"Got it, Roz. Not a problem." Joe tossed his napkin and a five-dollar bill onto the table and stood up to brush the bear claw crumbs from his uniform. "I'm walking back to the office right now. Just look out the window."

Disconnecting Joe, Roz returned to Augusta. "Hold one minute, sugar. Joe's headin' into the county building right now."

"Thank God. My cell battery's low and the signal's weak up here." Augusta's gaze mirrored the void of the mouth of the mine.

Through the window of her corner office in the county building, Roz scanned the street for Joe. There he was, walking under a brilliant sun that illuminated the gray flecks in his hair. At an altitude of over 10,000 feet, the sun was a bright and regular fixture that didn't necessarily equate with warmth. Although, it would likely hit the mid-sixties on that late August day, it already felt like they were into fall. The aspen leaves were starting their translucent fade. Nights were already too cool for the flowers to recover each morning. Late summer t-shirt clothed tourists were buying sweatshirts saying, "I got Higher in Oresville, Colorado."

At such an altitude, the clouds wouldn't hang around a full day. Mt. Massive, commonly called "The Massive" and peaking at nearly 14,500 feet, put up a jagged, rocky barrier that weak storm fronts usually couldn't surmount and, with a whimper, imploded. The big fronts hit The Massive and created a hook to the south where the Collegiate Peaks shouldered better possibilities. When conditions were just right, some fronts hit with more of a slice northward creating bragging rights for the ski slopes at Vail. The Rocky Mountains certainly worked better at staving off storms than the Gulf of Mexico where Roz called home in the bayous of Louisiana. *Enough with the Vitamin D report. What is Augusta gabbing about now?*

"Is this an election year, again, already?" Augusta went on. "I'm about four years behind. Seems like Joe just got elected. No wonder he was at the bakery—politicking again. Did I know this was an election year or is this another case of the news media inducing citizens' memory loss? The next time I see Garcia at the Elks Club, I think I'll deliver an impromptu verbal *Letter to the Editor* on the editor himself."

"Actually, I think elected officials are always campaignin'," said Roz, flexing her fingers to admire her freshly polished nails. "It's always about the next election, so your news about Al is not going to be particularly welcomed, if ya get my drift. You know Joe is not big on drama or anything close to serious crime. As for talking with Garcia about your editorial statement, I wouldn't recommend you ruin his limited leisure time at the Club— that is, if you can hold your thoughts. Wait, Augusta, Joe's comin' in the door now. Hold on, I'll transfer you."

Sheriff Joe Jackson picked up the call. "Augusta, what in the world is going on now? Last I heard you hadn't found your sixth husband." The sheriff always liked to tease Augusta about the number of husbands she was burning through, but this time there was no chuckle forthcoming.

"Better get up here quick, Joe. Al is dead. I'm at the Sunshine," Augusta's voice held strong.

Joe wanted to say, "Damn it, Augusta. I was having a pretty good day of it without this kind of situation. Now I'm probably going to miss lunch and afternoon break by the time I get up there." Instead, in his professional sheriffing voice, he announced, "I'll call my fav and only part-time detective, Deputy Phoebe Korneal, and we'll be along shortly. Given the road to the Sunshine is a rugged ATV forest service trail, it may take us a bit. Stay where you are, and don't touch anything, ya hear me?"

As he hung up the phone, Joe started thinking about all the work he imagined he had to do that day. As an elected official, there was always something to be done each day, and always something he had not counted on doing. In Joe's opinion, his undersheriff, Bill Diamond, was probably a better choice to go to the Sunshine with Phoebe and meet up with Augusta.

However, Joe speculated that if Old Al was dead, there might be a news story with a photo opportunity, and he wouldn't want to miss out on that. After all, the voting citizens of Green County needed to see their elected Sheriff in full control of the investigation into the unfortunate demise of Old Al Lewis, a longtime member of their small community. Regardless of his employment choice of Gold Prospector, he was still an Elks Club member. Or was he? If he was a member, why didn't he ring for entrance into the Club? No matter the answer to that question, he should still be respected in his passing. Perhaps an official Elks Departure Ceremony at the Club would be in order.

Sheriff Joe had been a supporter of the Club since he was a kid. Growing up in Oresville, the central focus of his formative years was the Boy Scout program, with an emphasis on earning the honor of Eagle Scout. Honor, being the foundation of character for an Eagle Scout, meant that

Joe lived it, breathed it, and thrived in the responsibility. "Honor as a way of life."

Joe's Eagle Scout badge came at age sixteen as a result of a community project for new carpet at the local Elks Club. The Club was the community space for weddings, funerals, holiday dinners, and a weekly Monday hamburger fry for a buck, or two burgers for an extra fifty cents.

At the time of Joe's Eagle Scout project, the Exalted Ruler and Manager of the Elks Club, Willie Friedrich, remarked, "The Elks Club is a nonprofit organization and will always prove to be a money loser. The new carpet coordinated by Eagle Scout, Joe Jackson, is proof we are *the community* to all ages, regardless of the legal age to drink!" The Club certainly wanted to support the Boy Scouts, not to mention receiving new carpet for the Club as part of that philosophy.

Joe called Phoebe at home. It was nine in the morning and he knew she was scheduled to work the two-to-ten evening shift. He thought he might need her thorough detective skills to make sure he didn't miss anything when they made it up to the Sunshine. Despite the banter about multiple husbands, he was bothered by the short talk with Augusta. He had a lot to do that day, but the death of Old Al? That was something he needed to tend to personally, as well as professionally. Let Bill Diamond cover the usual stuff while he and Phoebe figured out what happened. He sure hoped it was death from natural causes.

The phone rang at Phoebe's, and she set down her second cup of strong, black French Roast coffee to answer it. "Hi, Sheriff," she said. "What's up?"

"Just got a call from Augusta. She's up at the Sunshine mine, and she found Old Al up there, dead. I need you to go up there with me and check out the situation. Mind having a few hours of overtime?"

"Not at all, Sheriff. I'll be dressed and at the office in twenty-one minutes."

Phoebe filled her travel mug with coffee and surveilled the kitchen and living areas of her single-wide. *Everything in its place and a place for everything.* She let out a satisfying sigh and mentally adjusted her detective's thinking cap. *It's great working in Oresville. Sure beats the hassles in Salt Lake City. 10-5, Over and Out.*

PHOEBE

When Phoebe first came to Oresville from Salt Lake City, she was thinking it would be a short stay. Life had gotten a bit messy in Utah, and a cooling-off period was in order. Renting something, even a single-wide trailer home in a small subdivision just outside of town, seemed appropriately temporary. Seven years later, the trailer was still home for the most part, and she was still reminding people that it was a *rented* trailer house. *One should always be ready for the next opportunity when it comes along.*

The monthly rent on her temporary home had not seen an increase in all the years she had lived there, and the other residents on the property liked having a Green County Deputy Sheriff in the immediate neighborhood. During her elongated short stay, she had gotten used to lots of snow in the winter, no lawn to mow in the summer, and no garage in which to park her truck or store accumulated belongings.

From the beginning, Phoebe decided to leave the previous tenant's Christmas lights hanging on the front end of the trailer. They differentiated her single-wide from the others, saved both time and energy, and were festive year-round . . . *if* she remembered to plug them in.

The Tiny Town Mobile Home Court was located just as the highway became Main Street at the south end of Oresville. The large collection of 1960s and 1970s trailers were just the short side of vintage. There were over a hundred trailers, the streets all had names, the one intersection had a stop sign, and it was the most affordable housing in the county—a real plus for Oresville. With many mountain towns lacking reasonably priced housing for their citizens, the residents felt lucky to be there. Vacancies were rare.

At one time, The Court, as the property owner liked to call it, was a comfortable setting of miners' temporary log and homes in the shadow of Mount Massive. Forty acres of hard-packed dirt that only the hardiest of weeds and cacti could pierce made up the wide spot of high mountain desert land, providing a solid foundation for all. One could not walk out a door nor look out a window without seeing the mountain itself or its shadow, depending on the time of day.

A view that was a true inspiration for the miners who believed there would always be something to mine and mill.

The Court sported a Community Hall for receiving mail and buying various high-priced specialty items. It even hosted a small ad hoc bar backlit by a single neon light marketing "Hamm's Beer." In the earlier days, the Community Hall featured a ping pong table, but the balls, along with the comradery associated with the hall, were long gone.

Most days, Phoebe worked the evening shift. In preparation for Sheriff Joe's request for an earlier start time on that particular day, and some upcoming detective work, she braided her chestnut brown hair, threw on some jeans, hiking boots, and a somewhat official Green County Sheriff baseball hat. Her bulletproof vest fit snugly over her specially tailored, dark blue sheriff's shirt. Grabbing her Glock 22 and deputy sheriff's badge, she layered on the heavy official sheriff's jacket. With only one town in the huge area of over 380 square miles, coffee shops were few and far between, so the heavy-duty coffee thermos in her galley kitchen needed to be full at the start of each shift, ready for policing all of Green County. Deputy Sheriff Phoebe Korneal was armed and ready.

Phoebe's job as the senior patrol officer suited her just fine. She had gotten to know most people in the town of a few thousand, at least the ones who routinely came up for attention of some sort. The townspeople were mostly miners or those with a history of mining. Jobs and opportunities were mostly limited to the open-pit mine for Molybdenum—atomic number 42—or small shops on Main Street. The ski area outside of town helped employment numbers in the winter and gracefully melted come spring. Employment as a sheriff's deputy was one of the steadier jobs in Green County *and* it had benefits. Not a bad gig for a single woman in her early thirties, who was still considered a newcomer to that small town even after many years on the job.

Gold mining in Oresville started around 1860. Located just north of Oro City in the California Gulch of the upper Arkansas Valley, Oresville's history was a rich, deep backdrop to the town's daily operations. The history of mining, an anchor that is hard to break, was intensely revered in Oresville.

A decade after the short-lived gold bonanza in the 1860s, silver became the next mining heyday. Black dust swirled and settled everywhere. Life slowed considerably with gold having lost its luster until the black dust proved to contain lead and silver. That news brought the miners back. Small miners' cabins sprung up, and the area needed a name if mail was to be delivered. The new area became the town of Oresville.

In the humming mining town, employment numbers and community prosperity fluctuated with demand for moly, the amount of snowfall at the ski area, and the length of the tourist season as dictated by the weather. The citizens of the community were as sturdy as one would expect living at nearly 10,500 feet above sea level. The locals had nicknamed the altitude an even "10-5"—slight embellishments such as those were often provided by the oxygen-deprived citizens of Green County.

Phoebe and her best friend, Carrie Jean O'Brien, had grown up in Salt Lake City. The two of them spent as much time as possible at the O'Briens' house. Since Carrie Jean's parents were not home much of the time, she and her older step-brother, Bill, had the run of the neighborhood. Phoebe was all too familiar with absentee parents, and happy to have the company of her good friends on great adventures.

Rather than going to college right out of high school, Phoebe had decided to follow in her uncle's footsteps and become a cop. Her uncle encouraged her to use her height—just under six feet—and solid build to her advantage. Good old Uncle Bob considered her first-rate common sense to be her greatest asset for police work. That, and she relished being in control. Uncle Bob called it a "strong personality"—a kinder, gentler way of saying she wanted to be the boss. Perfect fit for a member of a police department. She signed up for the Volunteer Junior Police Department League and got a part-time job as a patrol dispatcher. On her twenty-first birthday, she took her police exam and passed with flying colors.

As a patrol officer, Phoebe had been occasionally on loan to the Special Crimes Unit in Salt Lake City. Patrol was always busy, but the patrol work became routine after the first few years. The crime rate in that ultra-clean city was slow and sporadic. The Special Crimes unit was even slower and somewhat undefined. Phoebe had tested high for the move up to the detective squad, and she was a solid detective when she did get an occasional Special Crimes temporary assignment. The odds of one of those becoming a permanent assignment for a woman were slim to none.

Disgruntled by social barriers standing in the way of her aspirations for a detective's shield, and disappointed by a broken romantic relationship, Phoebe put out a probe for a new job in a new location. Her Best Friend Forever, Carrie Jean, was already in Oresville and reported that "livin' high" in that small town would be a great opportunity—not only for their friendship, but also for their careers. Carrie Jean would have an insider for leads. Phoebe would gain back her BFF and revel in total liberation from her ex-lover. Both Phoebe and Carrie Jean had had enough of men for the time being.

The interview over the phone with Sheriff Joe went better than she could have hoped. She was hired as a deputy patrol officer and an occasional detective as needed. Elated, Phoebe announced to friends, family, and PD peers that she was leaving Utah to reboot her career in law enforcement. The police department was as happy to see her leave as she was to be leaving. A sparsely attended farewell party yielded a few women from the 911 bureau, and that pretty much said it all. "Goodbye, Utah. Hello, Colorado!" With all of her life and career experience packed in two suitcases, she pulled her silver Ford 150 into a shaded parking spot at the county building to start her new job in sleepy, little Oresville.

Little did she know back then how interesting that job was going to be!

RUGGED ROAD

G rabbing the thermos of coffee, Phoebe jumped out of the truck, righted her belt, and situated her vest. As she entered the sheriff's office, Joe looked at his watch and then at her. "Right on time as always, Phoebe. Thank you."

After six years as a deputy sheriff, Joe Jackson had become the elected and re-elected Sheriff of Green County. He liked to campaign. His speeches always began with, "I went from the basement as a janitor to the top floor as Sheriff. It was a rather circuitous route, but now I'm steeped in the needs of all people in this great county. *Vote for Joe!*" And the citizens of Green County did.

Born and raised in the Oresville community, Sheriff Joe had lived there his whole life, with the exception of one completed college year away from home. He and his wife, Mary Margaret—his "Sweet M&M" as Joe fondly referred to her—had taken the occasional vacation, but only a few days here and there. It was hard to take a vacation *from* the Rocky Mountains. Living there, they were surrounded by mountains peaking over 14,000 feet high (commonly referred to by locals as "14ers"), eye-busting green forests, high mountain lakes reflecting perfect blue skies, and streams featuring the elusive native Cutthroat Trout. Catching a "Cut" was a big event for the occasional fly fisherperson like Joe Jackson.

As Joe saw it, a career in law enforcement really dictated his constant attention. His dedication to law and order extended from the office to his own self-image and then to his family. Unfortunately for him, his wife and four daughters didn't share his expectations for *law and order* and everything working like clockwork according to his tightly organized, slightly obsessive schedule. Instead, his schedule existed within the confines of his own mind and no others, creating a frustrating struggle for him during his children's teenage years.

Having a similar obsession with time, Phoebe recognized punctuality as one of her professional standards. Present and ready for the journey into the unpredictable mountains, and decked in so many layers that Joe thought she looked like a tall beached whale, Phoebe trusted that she was well-prepared for work at the high altitude of tree line, even if it was August. Men are from Mars, women . . . well, not so much. Joe grabbed his own heavy sheriff's jacket and checked his badge and gun. The two of them nodded to Roz at the front desk as they headed for the motor pool.

Three minutes later, Joe and Phoebe were in the county's ten-year-old tricked-out Jeep Wrangler. The engine purred like a comfort animal, ready to spring into action. *It might be ten years old, but it runs like a charm,* Joe mused. Anything with a running motor and good tires had his affection. Thanks to his meticulous care, the old Jeep had become Joe's reliable favorite.

When your county covers almost four hundred square miles of Rocky Mountain terrain loaded with rocks, wild animals, and a forest of pine trees so thick it blocks all sunlight, you need to have the right vehicle to get you where you're going . . . and back home again. That was Joe's philosophy when it came to his daughters and their transportation needs. The girls were only a few years apart and always needed to be driven somewhere. It was a wonderful day when the oldest daughter started driving— though not quite yet at the legal driving age, which Joe viewed as only a *slight* bend of the rules to favor peace in his household—and found a part-time job to pay for her own gas.

Together, Joe and his oldest daughter had carefully selected a beat up 1970s VW bus for her to drive her sisters around in town. The boring beige would not show dirt or the scrapes and scars expected from having a teenage driver at the wheel. Joe's logic was that she would likely cover the bumpers with stickers—and with the help of her sisters, that did not take long. The four girls also proceeded to liberally apply several cans of blue spray paint. Blue was their favorite color and the VW was christened the "Blue Bus."

VW engines were easy to maintain, and Joe announced that he would teach each of the girls how to change the oil, check the spark plugs, add water to the radiator, and top off the windshield washer fluid. All of which they never did. Instead, Joe took good care of the Blue Bus.

When it came to the county vehicles, Joe made sure the annual budget had a line item designated for the necessities of mountain trail travel. He equipped the county's four-wheel-drive Jeep Wrangler with a sturdy high-end cattle guard across the front, a special Mammoth five-inch lift kit for the rugged terrain, a 9,500-pound winch, a max-powered spotlight that could be remotely operated, and a set of roof lights that could blind the biggest moose. And Rocky, said to be the largest bull moose in the state, was close at hand, roaming the mountains around Oresville.

As Joe and Phoebe headed north out of town, they made it quickly to the rugged trail leading to the Sunshine. Joe drove the Jeep onto the bumpy path just as Phoebe was sipping coffee from her thermos cup. "It should be easy to figure out what happened up there, Phoebe. Everyone likes

Old Al. No one would want to hurt him. Bet he just had a heart attack or something."

"Maybe so, Joe," Phoebe said as she mopped up the spill, "but until we know what actually happened, let's pay attention to this trail, the surrounding terrain, and any parking and camping areas along the way for anything unusual." As always, her suspicious detective mind took precedence over the assumption that nothing sinister had happened. "There might be someone or something that can give us a clue about what occurred in Al's final hours. What was Old Al doing at the Sunshine mine in the first place? And what was Augusta doing there?"

Phoebe shifted her thoughts to her career. *Old Al's demise could yield me a few days of detective pay, and maybe even move me into a fulltime detective's job if I handle this case in short order.*

Sheriff Joe appreciated Phoebe's gumshoe skills and training from her stint with the Salt Lake City police. He counted on her talents whenever there was sleuthing work to be done. Although he didn't anticipate the need for a fulltime detective for Green County, he knew that if his department ever needed one, Phoebe would be his first choice. The expense for a detective versus a deputy sheriff was, however, something he couldn't justify at that moment. He had learned to be critical of needless spending, especially during election time when it was important to consider the county's budget.

As Joe wrestled the Wrangler up the tooth-rattling trail to the Sunshine, he and Phoebe watched the road carefully for any signs of tracks made by a vehicle, animal, or human. The Jeep crept along successfully through ruts and over rocks along the shorter trail to the abandoned mine. Another smoother trail snaked in from the north, but it was much longer and time was of the essence.

"Looks like the runoff from the snows of last winter took its toll on this road. I don't think many of these rocks have ever seen the light of day. Just trying to get around them and stay on the road without ending up over the edge, is tricky. It's a steep drop-off here and we wouldn't ever be found," he added with a nervous laugh that did little to relieve the tension.

"I'm just bouncing around here, Joe, wondering if Old Al found something at the Sunshine, like gold or silver, and was up there in hopes to open it up again."

Joe shook his head, "The Sunshine mine was abandoned over a hundred years ago when the gold rush ended. When silver mining took over the mountains, the Sunshine jumped on the band-wagon. In most cases, silver mining proved to be a waste of prayers, hope, and money. Now the Sunshine is just a temporary destination for rock-crawlers and high-end ATV quads. It's at tree line and tough to get to. The weather is dicey and decent shelter is nonexistent in the winter at this altitude."

Phoebe questioned, "If that's the case, what was Old Al doing there?"

"Who knows what brought him there?" Joe pondered. "He was old. Case open and shut, just like the Sunshine mine. There you have it. What intrigues me is why Augusta is there instead of at her own mine, The Last Hurrah, which is only a few miles away and much easier to get to."

The two fell silent, mulling over the possibilities. Joe's cautious driving in granny gear was irritating but gave Phoebe the opportunity to watch the road and the tall pines on either side for anything that didn't belong. She knew the Wrangler was built and equipped with its off-road tires and huge engine to practically roar up the trail. Maybe she would insist on driving back down the mountain under the premise of giving Joe a well-deserved rest at the end of this long day. She figured she could use the practice driving that kind of trail anyway.

With her thoughts bouncing and drifting in time with the rocky road, Phoebe cogitated, "Old Al was called Old Al because, well, he's old! Hands down, he should have already moved into his winter digs. Weather'll be early this year. Hanging out at the Sunshine in late August is a little short-sighted. He should have known better. It looks like there has already been a dusting of snow up on the Massive."

Joe corrected her, "I don't think Old Al had a cabin at the Sunshine for spending winters there. Maybe he tried to live in the mine itself? Fact is, I've never thought about where he lives in the winter. I don't see him in town very often once the snow flies, so we can probably rule that out. Back in the day, most prospectors built themselves a cabin somewhere for shelter. In the new millennium, prospectors usually have a home in or on the outskirts of town where they spend the least favorable mining months of the year. Augusta should know where he hangs his hat."

Taking copious notes, Phoebe added that to her growing list of questions. "The Old Farmer's Almanac predicts even more snow this year than the usual 150 inches. This tells me the winter will be early and longer than any of the seven winters I've spent here. Everyone knows that winter can't deliver record snows if it gets started too late, right? When winter starts early, we get a little snow every day. And it never melts. Before you know it, there are snowbanks everywhere and no one can *see* the sidewalks, let alone *walk* on them. Speaking of snowbanks, I think we should be writing tickets this year for 'Failure to Clear Walkways.' There must be a law on the books somewhere that we can use. Have you ever thought about setting a goal for the number of tickets each deputy must issue each month? Never hurts to build the county coffers, you know."

"Phoebe, issuing snow-tickets isn't doable, and I don't know whether I put much stock in the Farmer's Almanac. It's printed before September every year. How can the weather be accurately predicted for the coming season? I suggest we focus on getting this investigation over with in time for an afternoon break." Spinning the

Jeep's wheels to jump a rut, Joe grumbled, "I wonder how in the hell Augusta got up here."

"We've been on the trail for an hour," commented Phoebe. "At this rate, lunch and an afternoon break will be in our dreams."

Joe ignored her. "Where is Bill Diamond, anyway? The Green County Undersheriff should be the one on this forest service trail, not the Green County Sheriff."

Phoebe didn't hear what Sheriff Joe was saying. She was more interested in the question of accuracy regarding the Old Farmer's Almanac.

How is it possible? she thought. *At a fifty-fifty chance of getting it right, those odds would probably be better than Punxsutawney Phil jumping out of the ground to see his shadow. Selling this as "accuracy" for nearly two hundred years? It's all marketing. Do people at this altitude even consider predicting weather with the Almanac?* She flipped open her notepad with a slap. *I wonder if Roz will be at the Elks Club tonight. She's been here longer than I have so she can advise us. When we get back to town, I can stop at the Club for a drink and some good old-fashioned gossip. Of course, we'll need Carrie Jean there for the juiciest tidbits.*

Joe had been on the county payroll long enough to have seen everything crime related, or even close to being crime-like, or even becoming a crime. His mind was a veritable mix of campaign mode and investigator mode while trying to keep the Jeep on the road.

He ruminated. *It's true that Old Al is just that—old. Augusta getting me up here is probably a complete waste of my time for just a routine death. She did sound worried, though. After burying three husbands, she does know death when she sees it. I wonder if I can get Jesús Garcia up here for a story. I could be interviewed and include a photo with my serious-all-business-look while I investigate. Cell service here is a remote possibility so radio might carry back to the office better.*

Shattering the silence, Joe grabbed the dash-mounted radio mic and buzzed Roz to see if she could at least roust Carrie Jean.

"Good Morning, we're having a great day at the Green County Sheriff's Office. Rosalind Marie Boudreaux speaking."

Joe sighed, "Roz, you really don't have to give this lengthy introduction when it's me calling. I already know your name and where I'm calling, okay?"

"It's all about being the professional that I am, Sheriff, regardless of the paltry pay I receive for being the coordinator for the *entire* department." When it came to money, Roz could have an edge, though her sarcasm given present circumstances surprised even her.

Already annoyed and feeling impatient, Joe leveled his voice, "I think we have already talked about your job description for this month, Roz. Coordinating the entire department, as you say, is not listed. Just focus on answering the radio calls and phone calls, please. Got it?

Should you be the next Green County Sheriff, your pay will still not be commensurate with the title. Can we move on?"

Roz had already moved on. "What do you need, Joe?"

"I'd like you to call over to Garcia at the Gazette and see if he is available—he's my first choice—or if not, can he get his reporter and photographer, Carrie Jean, out to the Sunshine? There is likely a story here for the citizens of Green County. See if you can find Undersheriff Bill and tell him to get up here to relieve me. I have important things to do today."

"Bill is on his way in, and Carrie Jean is headed that direction now. Augusta called her first, so she might already be up there. I'll tell Bill to radio you. Over and out." With that rather clipped, huffy close, Roz released the radio key, turned down the volume, grabbed her jacket, and stepped outside for a smoke.

Under the guise of getting some "fresh air," Roz allowed herself one cigarette every two hours while on duty and did not indulge when not on duty. A casual outdoor break at work gave her the opportunity to view the town's streets and schmooze with folks walking by. Of course, the weather had to be checked and citizens greeted. A casual cigarette was a well-deserved respite and could become a citizen alert should anyone be misbehaving.

The Sheriff's Department packed the full main level of the two-story County building on Gold Avenue, in the heart of downtown Oresville. There were always some people in the building for citizen business and usually some hanging around the main door looking for the latest news. The benevolent town council, several elections back, finally put two benches by the main door just to accommodate those interested parties.

Since the addition of benches, a food truck moved to a wide spot on the street. It offered a limited variety of local fare for citizens wandering around the Green County building, tourists vacationing on the main street of Oresville, and for those working in the building. With all that, plenty of lawn, and a few flower beds courtesy of the local Ladies Garden Club, the County Building was a good way to pass some time for the locals. Amid those happy sounds, there was always the possibility of a sheriff's patrol vehicle leaving the parking lot, practically spinning tires.

***

As the county's Wrangler carefully crawled up the side of the mountain, another vehicle came roaring up behind them. The sound was unmistakably the rumble and gurgle of an ATV 4-wheeler quad. Joe hit the brakes. The High Country Gazette's ace reporter, Carrie Jean O'Brien, in her usual hurry, rushing to meet Augusta at the Sunshine, came to a dead stop just before rear-ending the Wrangler. Sheriff Joe checked the rear-view mirror with mixed emotions. There stood Carrie

Jean, bouncing on the quad floorboards in an effort to see around the Jeep.

Joe stopped on the narrow path—narrow enough to ensure Carrie Jean could not pass—and both he and Phoebe got out of the Jeep. The steep drop-off on the right and a towering mountainside on the left would keep the young reporter in check and the sheriff in charge. Negotiating that trail was beyond the ability of the casual day-hiker, especially at that altitude with plentiful slippery scree to twist an ankle or worse. They stumbled along the rocky, rutted trail, alongside the Jeep, back to Carrie Jean, each taking a side of her ATV.

"I suppose you heard what we are looking at here, Carrie Jean?" Joe wanted to dissuade her from being too eager about the story, but first he needed to know what information she had already gathered.

She looked at Phoebe, "Morning, Phoebe. I thought you would have already seen Old Al and Augusta. What's the deal? How's about a statement?"

Phoebe rolled her eyes up and right and, with a slight smile on her lips, shook her head, meaning *not now, Carrie Jean.*

As usual, Carrie Jean was comin' in hot for the story. "Sheriff, I'm only looking to report the facts. Our readers are hungry for local news and I could do an online breaking news flash before noon! The Green County E-Blast! Whaddya say? How about you make a statement? Maybe an educated guess as an anonymous bystander? I'd take anything you'd like to say. Of course, I'd keep it short."

Ignoring Carrie Jean's request, Sheriff Joe assumed a more rigid pose and launched into his lecture.

"Since you're going to be at the Sunshine with us, Carrie Jean, let me forewarn you that when we get to the mine, I'm going to have to ask you to stay back. In fact, once we arrive, just stay on your vehicle while Deputy Phoebe and I check out the situation. When we have everything figured out, one photo will be allowed. And slow it down. Got it?"

Carrie Jean was not happy with his command. She had set herself a noon deadline, and she never missed a deadline. Usually. She was already plotting her Plan B. She definitely would not sit and wait—not her style. If anything, she would create news from innuendo. She had gotten an early call from Augusta that morning, who sounded upset, even mad about Old Al. Carrie Jean decided she would first interview Augusta while the sheriff and Phoebe looked things over. At least, if she was near the mine, she would be close enough to overhear their discussions.

Carrie Jean happened to be good friends with Augusta. Augusta never had any children in spite of five marriages and the practice it takes to produce children. She never had to hone the skills of parenting until she met the young reporter. Carrie Jean, on the other hand, had parents who were pretty much absent and usually on a variety of special mission trips for the church. The friendship between the two women was based on that parent-child gap. It was only natural that Augusta's first call that morning was to Carrie Jean.

With a wave and a hard, inconsolable expression to Joe, Carrie Jean revved up her ATV. Phoebe yelled over the engine noise, "Follow us the rest of the way, and stay behind far enough so we can hear ourselves think."

"Haven't been up here in a while, Phoebe," said Joe, watching the forest service trail ahead as he drove. It was theoretically a two-track trail, though too narrow in most spots for vehicles to meet and pass. The tops of the blue spruce, Douglas fir, and lodgepole pines on the drop-off side were close to the path. Some areas of the forest were too dense and dark for sunlight to see the ground—"dark timber." As he drove, there would pop a stand of aspens with thin, transparent green leaves looking ready to turn gold. He could almost smell the changes in the air forecasting an early fall.

"Last time I headed toward Mosquito Pass was last summer when I took a few hours off to go fishing. I wish my girls liked to fish, but at least they enjoy eating fresh trout. My Sweet M&M fries them up like nobody's business!"

Joe had been in his sophomore year in college when Mary Margaret arrived as a freshman. Their plan was to complete college, get married, and start a family. The best laid plans don't always work out. Joe's second year of college was a proportional challenge. His raging hormones and those of his sweetheart, the good Catholic girl, combined for near disaster. They were both still teenagers when the somewhat surprising news of their pregnancy was announced privately by her doctor. Joe had cheerfully told his Sweet M&M, "This is exactly what we've been planning except we thought it'd be some time later, like down the road, like when we could at least vote or buy beer! My Sweet M&M, the timing is a little off, but whatever! I love you and want to spend the rest of my life with you. So, let's get on with it now."

The couple had agreed that the order of planned events for their life together would have to be reversed. At age eighteen, who doesn't look at life with a short-sighted view? Finally, in their mid-fifties, their plan had worked out, and their four daughters were mostly launched into adulthood. Life was good at 10-5.

At that high altitude, the past winter's snow, wind, and run-off had cut deep grooves in the trail and exposed rocks never before seen. On top of that, there were always backcountry avalanches—a natural occurrence in the Rockies—some that made the news, others that didn't. Often a trail required weeks to clear the snow.

Every spring was a whole new adventure on the trails, and by late summer, the outdoor enthusiasts had made it even worse. It had been a busy summer with quads, motorcycles, and side-by-sides roaring from dawn to dusk. Hikers did not stand a chance.

The sheriff's Wrangler found no challenge there thanks to its new off-road tires. In four-wheel drive, with the off-road ridge Grappler tires dug in as needed, it was doing a fine job of negotiating the tough terrain.

Joe was driving more prudently than the urgency of the call from Augusta dictated. He intended to protect the vehicle and save his aching back. There would never be enough money in the county budget to replace the Wrangler, so Joe was going to make sure that vehicle survived his elected tenure. After all, he never knew when he might be able to grab a few hours, his fishing pole, and head for Half Moon Creek. "The mountains are calling and I must go," as John Muir is credited with writing. And Sheriff Joe Jackson certainly agreed with Muir's thinking, albeit calling to *Joe*.

CALL THE CORONER

It took longer than expected to arrive at the Sunshine, and when they did, it was not a pretty sight. Augusta's new, state-of-the-art, side-by-side, off-road UTV with a 1000cc turbo engine was parked haphazardly at the top of the trail next to the abandoned mine debris. Phoebe was surprised to see such a fully loaded machine. She had heard Augusta had bought something new, but *that* was over-the-top.

Something had obviously slid to a stop on the shale, mine tailings, and weeds. "Looks like Augusta must've slammed on the brakes here," Phoebe remarked. "She was certainly in a hurry. The driver's side door is open, and the five-point harness seat belt is hanging out."

Sitting behind the wheel, and looking over at the body, Joe shrugged. Old Al was splayed out on the dirt, face down. *Probably a heart attack,* he speculated.

Too close for Phoebe's comfort, Carrie Jean had practically been on the back bumper of the Wrangler the entire last mile. There was a jolt when Joe hit the brakes, but the airbags didn't go off, so it must have been lighter than it felt. *Did Joe hit the brakes so suddenly to purposely cause a rear-end accident?* she wondered.

Phoebe was pretty sure that Carrie Jean was not happy with what Joe had asked of her—or, more correctly, with Joe's *order* to stay back. Her childhood friend was an excitable, quick-tempered, red-headed, Irish gal in her early thirties with her own way of doing things—everything, including covering and reporting the news, or in some cases, creating "just the facts."

Standing next to the Wrangler, Phoebe scanned the mine site. She had never been all the way to the end of that trail and noted the beauty of nature hidden away there. The area around the entrance to the abandoned mine was dotted with scattered grasses and ground sedum. The small wildflowers helped to break up the hard, wind-blown area at the tree line. There were some hearty blue columbine flowers growing out of rocks, and in the distance stretched an alpine meadow looking golden in the dry days of late summer.

The mine appeared as forlorn as the dream of silver mining. The entrance was not deep. Instead, Phoebe could see collapsed timbers, piles of dirt blocking some of the opening, and the few remaining standing timbers ready to give way.

It was late August, and already a bit of snow was evident in the shade and on the mine tailings. *Must have snowed here this last week,* Phoebe noted as she took in the scene. She struggled to stretch her second jacket over her first. *It's still chilly in the late morning and probably froze overnight, and we're likely going to be here for a while.* Her ears tingling from the cold, she traded her baseball cap for the down-filled beanie. *Game on!*

Augusta was sitting in an old, rusty folding chair near the mouth of the Sunshine, staring blankly at the body of Old Al. Dressed in muddy hiking boots and a worn-out rancher's green jacket covered with black dust, Augusta perfectly exemplified the spirit of an expert mine owner— a strong-minded woman unafraid of the hands-on work. Her blue jean overalls were stiff with years of mixed dirt, clay, and mud. With a ratty, knitted, red hat pulled low to her eyes, she looked to be underdressed for the cool morning air.

Phoebe walked carefully around the edge of the trail, over the tailings, and around a few boulders to get to her. With her Special Tea in her left hand and an unlit cigarette dangling from the right, tears drifted down Augusta's slightly weathered face. She seemed not to notice Phoebe was even there.

Kneeling at her side, Phoebe wrapped an arm around the mining woman's shoulders. "Hey there, Augusta," she spoke softly in a low sympathetic voice. "This is a sad day. I know you and Old Al go back a long way. I'm so sorry for your loss. It's a loss for our town, too."

It was at that moment that Augusta seemed to acknowledge Phoebe's presence. Sitting up a little straighter, she took a deep breath and slowly exhaled. "Thanks, Phoebe. I came here to give Al a piece of my mind about how he treated Hank, but I never got the chance. I found him just the way he is, lying there, face down and cold as a stone."

Joe was still sitting in the Wrangler, surveilling the scene. *Augusta's side-by-side, a bit of snow scattered, the mine opening, scattered mine tailings thick with weeds growing over them.* Stepping out of the Jeep, he hiked up his pants, balanced the gun holster, snapped on a pair of rubber gloves, and followed Phoebe's footsteps to catch up to her.

"This is a sad state of affairs, Augusta. How long have you been up here?" he asked as he approached the two women.

"A couple of hours, Joe. Waiting on you."

As Joe talked with Augusta, Phoebe turned her attention to Old Al. There were no marks on him to be seen from where she was kneeling next to Augusta. She was looking over the area around Old Al's body and trying to comfort Augusta at the same time. Augusta's footprints, along with hers and Joe's, could be seen in the chalky dirt, but there were no other fresh-looking footprints around.

Augusta stared off into the distance, "I came over this morning at about nine, Joe. Just needed to have a talk with Al about the young man, Hank, he's been using as a sherpa. Yes, I've told him and told him to get some help. He's too old to be working all summer by himself. But Al knows better than to take advantage of kids wanting to learn, and instead just working them for little or no pay. Last night, the kid showed up at The Last Hurrah. I'm still camped there before winter sets in. After a snack and a soda, he told me the whole story as to what was going on with Al. *Now* what are we going to do?!"

Only half listening to Augusta's description, Joe stepped carefully over to the body to check for a pulse. There was none, and as Augusta had said, the body was cold as a stone.

"Probably just a heart thing or something, Phoebe." Joe's thoughts became words as fast as he could think them. "I guess we had better call for the coroner to come up here to collect Old Al. This is going to require a lot of work, and there goes the rest of my day. I think I'd better get Bill up here pronto. Wonder if Roz bothered to get him headed this way?"

Still trying to take care of Augusta, Phoebe decided first things first—*get her out of the way.* She motioned to the woman sitting there in an obvious state of shock, "Let's have you come over to the Wrangler and sit where it's comfortable. Joe and I have some work to do around here. Have you stashed some warmer clothes on your machine?"

Though Augusta seemed not to hear her, Phoebe helped guide her to her feet and walked her to the Wrangler.

Carrie Jean was off of her vehicle and had already taken several pictures of the scene with her phone-cam, in spite of Joe's admonishment of *only one photo*. She was trying to simultaneously stay out of the way and get closer to Augusta, too. As she walked up to the Wrangler on the driver's side, Phoebe shot her a look that said, *not now, Carrie Jean, get back to your vehicle*.

"But this is my friend and she called me for help." Carrie Jean whined. "I need to comfort her in this time of loss."

Phoebe looked down at her notepad and, with an unseen eyeroll, mumbled, "Just sit tight, please."

Carrie Jean stomped off in a huff. Grabbing a roll of yellow crime scene tape from the back seat of the Wrangler, Phoebe started taping off the area—more to keep Carrie Jean and Augusta out of the way than anything else. Her detective skills were a little on the rusty side. She needed to brush up her memory on where to start. There weren't many deaths she was called to investigate in that small mountain county. Actually, Old Al's was her first.

Joe returned to the vehicle and grabbed the radio mic to call Roz. He gave Augusta a reassuring look. "Leave it to us, Augusta. Old Al's demise will be priority number one. Right, Phoebe?"

"You bet, Joe," Phoebe chimed in, "and we're on it right now."

Augusta stared straight ahead, choking on her words, "Best thing you and Joe can do is find out what happened. I'm thinking maybe he tripped on all the rocks and tailings, fell, and hit his head. Maybe a heart attack, but he was as healthy as his worthless mule, Rose."

Phoebe's head snapped around. Where *was* the mule? Phoebe scanned the area again. If Rose had been there at the mine, where were her hoofprints? No Old Al footprints either. No sign of how he even got there. He never went anywhere without Rose and his prospecting rocker box. As she strung out the crime scene tape, Phoebe peered closer. It looked like the whole area had been brushed clean. Maybe there had been a strong wind up there overnight. If Augusta had brushed the area, there wouldn't have been any prints from her steps either, and that was not the case. Augusta's footprints, however, went right from her UTV over to the dead body by the rusty chair she was sitting on when they arrived. *What did they do, drop him from the sky?*

The scratchy connection threaded the sound of Roz's voice thinly through the radio's receiver. Joe gave her the order to send Doc Watson, the county coroner. "And did you call Bill and talk with him already?" he added.

"Yes," Roz replied, somewhat irritated that he doubted her ability to follow orders. "He came in shortly after you called. He knows what you're working on."

"Great, Roz. Make sure to have him come up here and relieve me. He can ride up with Doc to help us move the body. Over and out."

In a rush, Sheriff Joe slammed the mic back into the dash bracket and hoped he would not be stuck there all afternoon. Campaigning at tree line with a dead prospector was hardly his idea of a way to win an election.

ROUGH CUT DIAMOND

Bill Diamond was the undersheriff of Green County. He had been in Oresville for a few years since his nasty divorce in Denver, and it had mellowed him.

Just before he was born, Bill's dad had been killed in Vietnam. His mom had married again when he was in his early teens, and Carrie Jean became his step-sister. Bill was the fun guy in high school. Classes were easy for him. He was a middling athlete and everyone loved him, or at least liked him. All that was the perfect storm for entering into college at Regis University. "Hey, Denver, here comes Bill Diamond!"

Those first few months of freshman year bestowed a newfound freedom for the good-looking, politically-minded, young man-in-the-making, which proved to be intoxicating in more ways than one. In the end, he dropped out of college. While continuing to draw a monthly support check from home, he searched for a career path that included solid weekend parties and talented women. After a year or so, his parents back in Utah finally figured out he'd left school, and the checks stopped.

Bill's girlfriend at the time, Venus Davidson—or VD as her friends called her—dreamed she would someday be a beautician. Slouching together on the beer-stained sofa, they decided it would be a grand idea to have VD chop off his curly, blond locks. As it happened, he cleaned up well and headed to the thrift store to find a halfway decent, gently used black suit. Looking fine and proper, he marched into the Denver police headquarters to apply for a job.

After some fast talking and lengthy phone calls, he was escorted into the Chief's office where the old family friend greeted him with open arms. So did the Chief's daughter, Cynthia, who was enrolled in the Sturm College of Law at the University of Denver.

For Cynthia, the tall, blond, blue-eyed, fun guy was the right fit. He would also get her dad off her back about finding true love—or true lust, as the case may have been. Her parents gladly paid the bill for the big wedding at the Basilica in downtown Denver.

Within a few years, Bill had been promoted, Cynthia had graduated from law school and landed in the Denver District Attorney's office, and the happy couple had two children.

As a Denver police officer and son-in-law of the Chief, Bill moved up the ranks and was made Patrol Sergeant by the time he was in his late twenties. His son and daughter were growing, learning, manipulating the adults around them, and making like-minded friends. Family life was good. Though content in his dream job for several years, Bill envisioned becoming Deputy Chief at forty or so. In his mid-thirties, his career aspirations started to dim and then fell off the radar screen entirely due to some unforeseen conflicts of interest involving his wife.

Their divorce had not been the easiest or fastest process. Once all matters pertaining to dissolving the marriage were signed, sealed, and delivered, Bill decided it was time to move on. He worried about how the kids would fare through such a tough divorce, but teenagers only care about the newest video game, their raging hormones, and their friends at school. He needed a change of scenery, but wondered if the kids would want to go with him? They were happy living in the Washington Park area located conveniently right across the street from the park. Who in their right mind would want to leave all that?

Knowing Bill's situation, Carrie Jean had told him about the gainful employment available in Oresville. The Sheriff's Department had several immediate openings. Two officers had moved down the road to Buena Vista and another to Salida. Bill saw Oresville as the hideout he needed that would give him some space, a chance to refocus his life, and the thin mountain air that would be the right medicine for his fried emotional state. He figured he could take up jogging again, work out regularly at a gym, get back to some hunting in the mountains, and forget women for the rest of his life. Oh, the joys of divorce.

Oresville welcomed him. Sheriff Joe welcomed him. Carrie Jean was thrilled to have her step-brother close. When Phoebe arrived, it felt like the old neighborhood gang had reunited.

While Joe and Phoebe were up on the mountain scouting out the crime scene, Roz updated Bill on everything she knew about the situation at the Sunshine mine. He assumed it was probably a natural cause of death. After all, the guy was called Old Al because he was, well, old.

It was a beautiful fall day at 10-5, and Bill decided the ride into the mountains would work just fine for him. He had spent some extra time in the county employees' gym earlier that morning and was feeling the monotonous ride to the mine would give him time to relax. Grabbing his phone, he called Doc Watson and arranged to ride shotgun with him, quite literally, ammo and all.

CHEST OF GOLD

The wind was topping the mountain peak and sliding down like an avalanche toward the Sunshine mine. The chill of it made the air feel like November, not August. At the tree line, there weren't many trees, bushes, fences, or otherwise, to tie off the yellow crime scene tape. Instead, there were rocks, weeds, alpine flowers, and scrubs in abundance, which in late summer were drying out in preparation for a long winter at nearly 12,000 feet. Feeling the cold penetrate her many layers of clothing, Phoebe quickly taped off the area. Where there was nothing substantial to attach the tape, she piled up several small rocks and wound the tape around them.

Squeezing her quickly cooling hands into a pair of latex gloves, she tugged the heavy-duty booties over her Sorels. Tracking a grid around the body, she worked her way across the general area, looking for anything that didn't belong. *Even if Old Al had died of natural causes, best to be on the safe side,* she thought, always aiming to follow professional procedures.

A piece of red yarn waved in the wind from where it was caught on a prickly weed. Pulling her cell phone from her pocket, she took a photo and bagged the evidence. It was pretty well worn and ragged, much like Augusta's hat. Soon, she spotted some narrow tire marks on a flat sandstone rock. The rubber marks did not look like something from a UTV, and they looked fresh. Tires on a side-by-side were wide and chunky. She called to Joe, who walked over to check the marks.

"These really don't fit with the usual tires at this altitude, Joe, although one never knows," she noted, pointing to the tracks

"They look like they could have been made by a trail bike," Joe commented. Pulling his ear, pursing his lips, and raising his eyebrows, he brushed the dirt from his gloves and walked back over to the mine opening.

Phoebe snapped a photo of the tread marks, just in case. Continuing to check for minute clues, she spotted what looked like the butt of a small cigar sheltered in a hollow between two rocks. Augusta smoked regular cigarettes, so it wasn't hers. *Actually, I've seen her with a cigarette many times,* she thought, *but I've never seen her smoke it, so maybe it's just a prop.* She recalled that Al didn't smoke at all. Or at least she assumed so, since she had never seen him smoke at the Club or anywhere else in town. *So where did this come from? Too recent to be last week's debris.*

The mine had been long abandoned, and camping above tree line was never one's first choice. The wind was crazy up there. It was always cool and too rocky to pitch a tent—*and* most campers would know better than to play with matches in such conditions.

Phoebe stepped over the crime scene tape and headed beyond the tire-marked rock. Sure enough, after a few minutes of looking, she found another small brown cigar butt.

"Do people still smoke these small cigars?" she mumbled to herself. "More evidence, but no real clues."

Joe knelt next to Old Al's body while Phoebe took notes. Face down in the dirt, Old Al was indeed dead as dead gets. He checked the body for obvious signs of the cause of death, being careful not to turn it over before the coroner arrived. From his angle, there was no blood or other signs of struggle. Joe was obviously thinking it was probably a natural death.

Still, some things did not add up for Phoebe. There were no footprints, human or otherwise. No signs Old Al was even there, other than his body. Where were his footprints? Where was all his camping equipment? Where was Rose? Phoebe was getting a gut instinct this was more of a crime scene than she had originally thought.

They all heard the coroner's truck before they saw it. As it crawled up the trail, the slow grinding of the engine sounded almost as ominous as the rest of the scene appeared. Phoebe climbed into the Wrangler to move it out of the incoming path. Beside her sat Augusta in the passenger seat, so still and silent that Phoebe thought she might be asleep.

"It's going to be okay," she assured Augusta. "You going to be alright?"

"As alright as I can be under the circumstances," answered Augusta.

"I'm going to go talk to the coroner now. I'll have Carrie Jean come keep you company." With a comforting glance toward the dazed woman, Phoebe exited the vehicle to greet Doc Watson and Undersheriff Bill.

The Green County Coroner was an elected position, no credentials required. Doc Watson had served for nearly twenty years. He was also the only mortician in town and not a medical doctor. The "Doc" title was a courtesy, as he was always readily available for consultations in the small town of two thousand residents where deaths were few and far between.

Doc stopped the truck at the end of the trail and maneuvered around so the back of the truck bed was positioned as close to Old Al as possible without disturbing the scene. He had already heard via the local grapevine that

Old Al had a heart attack. How people had already diagnosed the cause of death without an autopsy was beyond comprehension. Gossip was not his favorite human trait . . . unless it served the investigation. But he could see how the town's folk might speculate—Old Al was, well, old.

Bill Diamond and Doc Watson had a good time coming up the mountainside. Doc appreciated the company during the ride. He could always use a helping hand, and a skilled storyteller was a bonus. Each had lived in other towns before Oresville. They had a shared history of short college careers, wonderful women, disinterested kids, and bitter ex-wives without alimony.

Joe stepped lightly over to talk with Doc and Bill. Meanwhile, Phoebe finished up the grid-search with next to nothing for clues. She asked the newcomers if they had brought any coffee or food. When they had started up the trail, the assumption had been a natural cause of death, but it had been a long morning full of growing questions.

At tree line, dehydration was common after an hour, so carrying water was a no-brainer. She and Joe had plenty of water, but no edible provisions. Doc was also used to a quick trip when called to any crime scene, so he typically didn't need to bring any food. As the morning dragged on, it became evident that no one had anticipated the length of time it would take for the ride up to the mine. And they still had to complete the investigation. Stomachs rumbled in stereo.

"What d'ya have here, Joe?" Doc asked.

Phoebe took center stage as she began describing the scene. "Doc, we don't have much and this is the problem. No clothes, no camping gear, no rocker box or his other mining equipment, no footprints, and his mule, Rose, has gone missing or was never here. It's almost like Old Al was dropped from above—not camping or mining up here like we expected."

Joe chimed in, "I'm not seeing anything on his body. No marks. No cuts. I was thinking natural causes. The body is cold so likely has been here a while. Augusta found him here early this morning. She called Carrie Jean first and then Roz. We came up straight away."

Both Bill and Doc put on heavy-duty paper booties to cover their boots and walked over to Old Al.

Doc was a stickler for detail when it came to death. "I'm thinking we'll need an autopsy to be sure it's natural causes. After all, he was called Old Al because he was, well, old. But if you two are thinking it looks sketchy, we better be sure on this and call the medical examiner."

He first felt for a pulse on Old Al's body to be completely certain he was dead. Then a quick body temperature check, as well as the temperature of the ground around the body. Though the freezing overnight temperatures made it hard to tell how long Old Al had been deceased, the medical examiner would need his measurements for a *guesstimate* as to time of death. Never a precise call at that altitude under those conditions.

Doc noted that Old Al was not wearing his usual mining clothes, but was, in fact, dressed for summer fun, not work, and certainly not for the cooling oncoming season of fall.

Phoebe turned to Joe, "I'll put in the call and ask her to be on stand-by. We'll be bringing in Old Al's body for an autopsy."

Doc and Bill got the stretcher and a fresh body bag out of the truck bed. Phoebe then used her phone to take additional photos of the scene. Bill, Doc, and Joe started to lift and turn the body to lie face-up on the stretcher.

Just as they did a one-two-three-*lift*, Phoebe spotted something shiny beneath Al's chest and yelled, "Stop!"

Someone dropped the legs. Another dropped a shoulder, and Joe was left holding Old Al's head and the other shoulder, which he dropped last.

Joe yelled back, "What the hell?"

Phoebe stepped over to the body and pointed, "Something there—under his chest." She told the men to turn Old Al on his side, and bent down to touch the shiny object. Stopping short of touching it, she waved back their hovering faces. "Hold it," she cautioned, put up her phone, and snapped some photos. Then she carefully picked up the item. It was a shiny, gold coin.

Phoebe examined the coin and showed it to the others who squinted to see its tiny lettering. Finding a gold coin in those parts was unheard of since about 1933 when President Roosevelt recalled those coins from public circulation. In the midst of a deep depression, hoarding gold coins was thought to be a problem for economic recovery. The solution was to turn them over to the government. Of course, all that was ancient history in 2015, but finding a coin under a dead body at an abandoned mine was either a clue or a tough coincidence to explain.

Gold coins in the mining business had a history of their own. Joe's grandparents had told him the Oresville stories about gold coins circulating in the 1860s. They served a real purpose. At first, the miners would put their gold into pouches and use a bit of gold dust to trade or purchase the few things they needed. The shopkeepers would take "just a pinch" for goods purchased. It was a very imprecise method of payment and fraught with temptation for even the most God-fearing businessman. A shopkeeper with big hands had an advantage in the gold dust exchange, since his larger "pinch" would garner a bit more gold than needed to cover what was owed. Women-owned businesses were prized by their customers, as the payment lessened with the size of their smaller hands.

Enter some clever men, the two Clark brothers and Emanuel Gruber. After a good deal of research, they determined it would be legal for them to mint their own gold coins. They started turning gold dust, flakes, and nuggets into coinage in Denver in 1860, creating $2.50, $5.00, $10.00, and $20.00 coins. In 1863 those entrepreneurs sold their equipment to the federal government, and the US Mint and Assay Office in Denver was born. By 1866, the gold had run out in the California Gulch near Oro City, and the gold mining business came to an abrupt halt. Oro City fell into steep decline. A few years later, silver was discovered. Both Oro City and gold coins were long gone. Down the road from the ghost town of Oro City, Oresville had been born in the arms of the silver mining boom.

In the light of midday, Phoebe, Joe, Bill, and Doc stared at the coin. It looked too clean to be from the 1800s and was definitely not a government-issued coin. The edge of the coin was smooth, though not perfectly round, and about the size of a fifty-cent piece. Stamped in fine print were the words THE LAST HURRAH, and fine lines burst like rays of sunshine behind the lettering. On the other side were stamped the numbers "2014."

"This looks like it was created with a half-ass amateur coin process," noted Phoebe.

Bill agreed, "You're right. And who tries to make their own money? It isn't legal, so why bother? And what's it doing under Old Al's body? I'd bet it belongs to Augusta. The Last Hurrah is her mine and she's the one who supposedly found him."

All four of them turned and looked over to the sheriff's Wrangler where Augusta had been seated. However, she was not there now. Neither was Carrie Jean.

As is said in politics, "It's not about the crime, it's about the cover up."

Extra! Extra!

Carrie Jean slowly slipped off her ATV, carefully negotiating the rugged ground as she made her way over to the Wrangler where Augusta sat in stunned silence contemplating Al's demise. Even the arrival of the noisy coroner's truck didn't seem to register.

"Augusta, let's go over to your ride and talk a bit." Carrie Jean took hold of her hand and guided her out of the Wrangler and over to the expensive-looking UTV. Obviously, Augusta had some appreciation for the finer things in life. Where else would you see a UTV tricked out with side doors, side curtains, a split windshield, and a heater?

Once they were out of the wind, Carrie Jean was more comfortable. She had ridden up the trail on her two-up quad that offered no protection from the wind, which set her teeth to chattering. She was dressed for neither late summer nor trail riding. In the sunshine, her ski jacket over a t-shirt was enough to keep her warm, but the cold wind in the shade was not as friendly. Standing there in her usual "Go Rockies" baseball cap, with black leggings bunching into a pair of canvas flats, her short frame threw a warped shadow across the UTV.

Carrie Jean hopped into the passenger seat. Augusta started the fancy machine, heater blasting welcome warm air onto their feet. The reporter was ready to get the facts and *just* the facts from her friend, Augusta.

Being careful not to sound interrogating, Carrie Jean coaxed her friend to tell her everything that happened that morning. However, instead of giving some insight into the actual events, Augusta went off about Al. In a raised voice and talking fast, she burst out, "I told him and told him he needed some help early in the spring on through the summer. We're not getting any younger, and he could afford to get some help. Then, this young kid appears on the scene and Al promises to help him become his own man. Mining is tough and placer mining, well, it's the worst. I told him and told him." She then drew in a big breath, put her fist over her mouth, and let out a slow, shaky exhale while a single tear inched down her face.

Who is this young kid she's talking about? And she's not calling Old Al "Old Al." She calls him Al. Just Al. The more Carrie Jean thought about it, the stranger it seemed. *And why was she lecturing him about getting some help? What was going on with her and Old Al?*

"So, what do *you* think happened to Al up here?" Carrie Jean used her "long pause" technique to give Augusta a chance to speculate.

Augusta, focused on the moss growing on the north side of the closest pine tree, slowly shook her head.

Carrie Jean tried again, "Augusta, when you called me this morning, you said Al was dead. How did you know? What brought you over here from The Last Hurrah?"

Augusta shifted her eyes away from the pine tree moss and turned to meet Carrie Jean's gaze. "Given I heard what Hank had to say when he stopped at the Last late yesterday afternoon, I thought I'd better have a little talk with Al. There's three sides to every story, ya know."

Carrie Jean looked perplexed at the "three sides to every story" comment. *And who is this "Hank" character?* she wondered. Having half-filled her notepad with plenty of so-called facts, she decided she had enough for her afternoon E-Blast! She'd catch up with Augusta later, but for the moment she needed to find a cell signal before the sheriff, who had explicitly asked her to be patient for a change, caught her interviewing Augusta.

Out of the blue, Augusta added, "I just can't imagine anyone wanting to hurt Al, never mind kill him."

Carrie Jean was shocked back into her seat. What did Augusta mean by "*kill* him?" Carrie Jean had assumed natural causes, and earlier, Augusta had mentioned maybe he tripped and hit his head on something. She had also assumed Al was dead when Augusta got there, *but was he?* Why would Augusta think someone had killed him? Well, the facts were the facts, albeit rather confusing, so that's the way she would report it. Sketchy at best. She could still come up with some kind of fresh-off-the-press news item. Those were the facts, or at least enough juicy tidbits to make a solid E-Blast! headline that afternoon. *Pulitzer Prize, here I come!*

Carrie Jean put her hand on Augusta's shoulder, "Just let this pass," she said in a comforting voice.

Augusta nodded her head and looked away. She was wringing a napkin in her hands while Carrie Jean shuffled off in search of her cell signal.

When Carrie Jean had first moved to Oresville, the quickest way to establish her new contacts was to join the Elks Club. It was at the Club that she met Augusta Ledbetter. She respected Augusta's knowledge of the history of the mountains and mining. Augusta loved telling Carrie Jean about her family history dating back to the mid-1800s, and Carrie Jean loved hearing about it.

Despite the twenty-plus years between them, they were a match made in heaven.

The job as the only reporter and photographer for the local paper, the High Country Gazette, wasn't necessarily her dream job, but it would give her a chance to prove her skills as a reporter. The editor, Jesús Garcia, wanted to breathe new life into how the news was covered, and Carrie Jean seemed like a good fit.

Growing up in Salt Lake City, her teachers used the politically correct, friendly term "inquisitive" to describe Carrie Jean's personality. One could say it was built into her genes. At home, she constantly asked "why" to the point that her parents simply ignored her. If they did answer, it was as if a totally different question had been asked. The answer would be a one syllable word given with one eyebrow at a peak. The eyebrow was meant to exhibit an astounding reply by the parent answering. After it was certain that Carrie Jean would not outgrow her inquisitive nature, the lifted eyebrow by itself was the standard response and usually enough to satisfy her unceasing string of questions and send her marching off in a new direction.

In her late teens, while friends were pursuing adulthood, promising long-term careers, and raging out of control hormonal satisfaction, Carrie Jean was focused on gossip of any kind. She rebranded the gossip as "news reporting" in her occasional blog. This became a way to make a living for a person who was nosey by nature. Her early adolescent rehearsal for the part of "reporter" led to a solid career in adulthood for Carrie Jean, leveraging her naturally occurring inquisitive nature.

She found her way into the business of reporting the news, or what could become news, at a local level. She was certainly not tall enough or slim enough to be a television newscaster, so the next best thing was a newspaper journalist.

Through a series of false starts, the newly turned twenty-five-year-old Carrie Jean landed in Oresville at the High Country Gazette. She was the only employee and, therefore, the star reporter. The "E-Blast!" was her baby, and she made damn sure it hit the e-stands every day in the early afternoon, even if it carried just the current weather report. She always kept her cell phone handy for photo opportunities and garnered lots of byline credits as a result.

The town was the right size for her to keep tabs on everything happening or going to happen. At times, she could circle back to a story for a follow-up. The relaxed, comfortable small-town culture lent itself to easy movement for a single gal. The mining history of the area was a constant source of information, and the re-telling of it brought a new depth of respect for the durable, long-standing citizens living there. All of that, combined with her freedom to gossip under the guise of reporting, made Oresville her top choice for a new home away from home. *What's not to love?*

And there was Carrie Jean on such a beautiful August day, shivering above tree line while gathering intel on the death of Oresville's beloved miner, Old Al. Faced with a pristine-looking death scene at the end of a trail, and her friend, Augusta, not wanting to talk or come clean with any details, Carrie Jean swung her leg over the seat of the quad and turned it around to depart the scene. It was doubly disturbing to her that her other friend, Phoebe, busy trying to do the job of a detective, seemed to be avoiding her as if she were just some local reporter. With all of that rumbling around in her head, Carrie Jean struggled to keep her mind on steering the quad around rocks and ruts on her way down the mountainside in search of a cell signal.

The whole situation was a mess, in her opinion, and not looking good for Augusta. Or maybe that guy, Hank, was the one she needed to talk with about Old Al. She already had a hunch on her Plan B—get the afternoon's E-Blast! on its way, go over to The Last Hurrah before anyone else arrived, and talk with Hank. She halfway agreed with Phoebe that it was probably death by natural causes, but an assumption too soon was a dangerous fork in the road. She was well aware of what happens when you "ass-u-me."

HIGGINS WOMEN

Augusta, born at the Oresville hospital in the early sixties, was a third-generation miner and an astute businesswoman. The inheritance of The Last Hurrah mine, along with the many businesses of her ancestors, left her financially stable. And it all began with The First Hurrah mine near Oro City where her great-granddad had first discovered gold.

Augusta's great-grandfather, Sam Higgins, had left Omaha when he turned seventeen. Intent on not living on the Missouri River, his goal was to expand the family business into whatever the New West would offer. Instead, he got wrapped up in the search for gold—Gold Fever—

and found the first gold nugget in the area that came to be known as Oro City.

That huge nugget weighed fifteen ounces. He had the gold assayed, sold it for $20.67 per ounce, and started his mining operation. That was back in the day when sugar was five cents a pound. In 2015, the value of that one nugget would have brought him nearly $10,000.

Great-grandpa Higgins was living large in 1860. That was the beginning of The First Hurrah mine. He built a one-room log cabin in the middle of nowhere, far from the mining operation. It was in a high mountain meadow of grasses in what would become a stand of aspens a hundred years later. After adding some basic furniture and outfitting the kitchen, it was "home"—a place to start a family. So, he jumped on his mule and rode over to a neighboring gulch to ask Miss Molly McDunn to be his bride.

He always knew Molly was the one for him, and she felt the same way. She agreed as soon as the question was out of his mouth. Molly was from a ranching and mining family out of Idaho Springs. She knew what to expect as a miner's wife, and she could clearly see that Sam, whose money was made in livestock trading on the Missouri River, had what it would take for them to build a successful life together. Married by the Justice of the Peace in Oro City, they settled into their one-room cabin and looked forward to a life of children, mining gold, and leadership in this small, developing town.

Molly started the Catholic Church outside of Oro City. The land was practically free at a dollar an acre if sixty acres were purchased, so she bought up sixty acres for the discount. She figured the church could sell off parcels of land as the area grew, thus becoming self-funding.

Locating the building outside of the town was an economic advancement decision by Molly. One weekend, the townsfolk pitched in to build a road to the church, and with a road and a church in place, cabins and a school soon followed.

Once the church bell was in place, she realized she needed a resident priest; however, Denver in the 1860s was a wild, self-centered town, and the visiting bishop too busy to read her letters of request. Without waiting for their solution, Molly put on a sturdy pair of miner's cotton pants, rounded up her horse, and rode down to the diocese in Santa Fe, New Mexico.

The bishop in Santa Fe admired her conviction. He listened to her descriptions and was appalled by her stories of mining, whores, and the lawlessness of the emerging mountain town in the New West. He agreed to send his able-bodied assistant, Father Joseph, to serve as their priest.

All the worship and church social life was thanks to Molly. Her strong-willed dedication to the community, undying faith in a heavenly presence, and desire for somewhere to go every Sunday morning kept the church strong. Even the mining town whores needed a place to gather on Sunday morning when business was at its slowest. The community of Oresville was blossoming.

Both Sam and Molly understood mining and the disappointments it could bring. When the gold petered out, they switched to copper. They named their new mining claim "The Second Hurrah." When the copper fizzled out, they switched to silver, and the new mining claim "The Last Hurrah" was born.

With three children, Sam and Molly still lived in the log cabin. They added a room each time another child came along. The youngest of the three was Augusta's grandmother, Constance Clark Higgins. Constance Clark was named in honor of Sam's mom who lived in the bustling town of Omaha, Nebraska.

Constance, or "Connie" as she liked to be called, became the mine owner as a teenager when an epidemic of diphtheria swept through the gulch's small community and took her family from her. It was believed the diphtheria was brought to the area by the railroad survey workers. Connie, staying with cousins for the summer in the area that later became known as Idaho Springs, somehow managed to dodge the bullet. She abandoned the cabin of sad memories and returned to Oresville for some male companionship. The wealthiest woman, albeit a young one, that side of Mosquito Pass, Connie was tough enough to handle it all.

As the years passed and the mining continued to pay off, Connie managed and expanded the Higgins' family businesses while buying up mountain property and water rights during the Great Depression. She bought several large brick buildings on Main Street in downtown Oresville and continued to grow the mining operations. The news of prohibition was welcomed, as she was already farming crops of barley and wheat—the stuff of bootleg liquor—in the remote mountains. There were plenty of skilled, out-of-work men who welcomed gainful employment—legal or not. Food on the table and a roof over their heads was what counted in dire straits.

All of that history contributed to the favored status of the Higgins' legacy. Connie ignored the original family business in Omaha as long as the old money was secure, safe, and growing over the long-term. Shrewd enough to protect the family assets, her one husband never knew the extent of her real wealth. The only good thing to come out of that brief marriage was one child, Anne Louise.

Anne Louise married more than her fair share of miners and local professionals, and outlived them all. Annie, as the townsfolk called her, ran the mine and all the other businesses single-handedly after her mother passed away. She started another family business of cattle ranching in the Oresville area. When Annie's only child, Augusta, was born in the 1960s, Annie incorporated all of the businesses.

In the 1980s, Annie turned all of the Oresville businesses over to Augusta and went off to Europe with her new companion, "Uncle Quinton." Together, they would see the sights of Europe and ride the Orient Express across the Asian continent. They eventually settled in Port-en-Bessin, Normandy, France. Their absence left Augusta in charge at the age of twenty-three, repeating the family's history of creating independent, wealthy women.

Like her grandmother and mother before her, Augusta had become one of the wealthiest women west of the Missouri River. And, like the Higgins women before her, she let the third generation of family lawyers manage her businesses back in Omaha. Those citified corporate attorneys made it a point to never have a need to visit her in the backwoods mountain town of Oresville.

Augusta also represented the essence of an independent mountain woman. She camped and hiked the mountains in the sun-drenched summers, skied the backcountry powdery snows of winter, controlled the mining operation, and managed to marry five times—having married one of her husbands three times. "Third time's a charm," she liked to laugh. Unfortunately, the third-time marriage with "husband number four," as she called him, was too much. He passed three months later, followed by a faux funeral at the Club for "husband number five" just a year and a half after that.

The mining operation soon became a hobby of sorts. She found significance in the name "The *Last* Hurrah," as she had no survivors to take over when she retired, should that ever happen.

The family's homestead cabin and surrounding 640 acres of land were privately held by Augusta and her absentee mother. The Elmira Wood cookstove worked like a dream. The outhouse was only a problem in the winter when the door froze shut. Constant use of the large hand pump kept the well-water flowing clear. Of all the cabin's fine features, the wood-burning stove was great-grandpa Higgins' pride and joy. It was top of the line back in 1860. He had ordered it with the optional nickel Victorian trivet attached at the back of the cooking surface. The front legs and skirt were also shiny nickel—all to impress his blushing bride.

The stories Augusta loved telling were the various iterations of the outhouses for the cabin. Over the past hundred and fifty or so years, several adaptations of an outhouse had been buried, moved, designed, burned, and rebuilt. One of them burned to the ground, thanks to sparks from a small fireplace in such a confined wooden space, combined with the incendiary fumes left behind from those longer "study" periods.

Even with those amenities, the cabin was too rough for Augusta's tastes and was too far from The Last Hurrah for her to live there. She preferred the creature comforts of her grandmother's house in Oresville. Al was dependable as the winter caretaker for the mountain cabin. For many years, she had let him spend his winters there, as long as he would repair any fallen timbers, chink the logs, patch the roof, and close off the seldom used rooms. He reported back to her each spring.

The one narrow track into the cabin was full of weeds and rocks, well camouflaged from inquisitive eyes. Al had posted "No Trespassing" signs deep in the aspen grove to discourage any hikers or hunters that might wander onto the property, but no one ever ventured up the overgrown, hidden path.

Al and Augusta had a working relationship based on their mutual interests in mining for gold and silver. Though their friendship was rock solid, no one ever suspected that they also had a straightforward business relationship—a contractual agreement based solely on an old-fashioned handshake and trust.

Thanks to her great-grandma Molly, grandmom Connie, and mom Annie, Augusta was a well-versed, solid business-woman. She appreciated living in Colorado and using the mountains to the max. Needless to say, she did not see herself as a nature nut. Concerned, yes . . . unless there was money to be made. She operated with a philosophy of being a contributing member to the community of Oresville, as one never knew when benevolent actions within the community could become a business opportunity. Leverage it forward!

The situation with Al's passing came as a genuine surprise to Augusta. Al was pretty much a loner kind of guy, although she suspected he had abandoned his wife many years ago to pursue his mining dreams. The fact that he would even take on the kid, Hank, was a shock, as she was sure he would not admit to the fact that he was getting old.

With each summer of prospecting getting tougher and tougher, Augusta prayed that their business partnership would continue in spite of the aging of the two of them. Seeing her friend, Al, lying there lifeless certainly put an end to her high hopes.

EMPTY POCKETS

As Joe, Bill, Doc, and Phoebe all stood up, they heard Carrie Jean taking off on her quad. The sheriff had been looking forward to a short interview for the E-Blast! and a photo op, but Carrie Jean seemed to have forgotten her duty to the citizens of Green County.

Feeling like there were too many moving parts to the story made Phoebe want to hit the pause button so she could catch up with her own thoughts about the sequence of events. She asked the men to leave the body right where it was while she had a talk with Augusta. More details were needed before Doc could haul the body down the mountainside. It looked like death by natural causes, but the coin was questionable. "The Last Hurrah" and "2014" stamps on it were odd—definitely not made at the mint, and why only one coin? Why not others if it were payment or re-payment for something?

Old Al's body was dressed in 501 Shrink-to-Fit Levis that could be tagged older than dirt. In lieu of a belt, he had strung a rope through the loops. Phoebe wondered what gyrations he would have had to go through if nature suddenly called. The rest of his attire was equally unusual— an oversized Hawaiian shirt, a John Deere ball cap, and a pair of leather cowboy boots—all obviously clean and from the spruced up side of his wardrobe. *No jacket?* Patting down his front and back pockets, she found no other coins. Nothing else there either.

Thinking out loud, Phoebe calculated, "Nothing in any of his pockets. No money, no matches, no keys, no Chapstick. Everyone in this state carries a Chapstick, sometimes two. Of course, living in the great outdoors, what would he need keys for? And what about the coin, and why just one?"

Bill looked at her and slowly shook his head. He had no clue either.

Standing with her notepad open, Phoebe looked around the area where the body lay. A grid search had yielded very little. What she had found, she had properly bagged and photographed, but they found no more coins. The cigar butts were unusual and looked recent. The grid was suspiciously clean . . . maybe it had been purposely cleaned. She took another look at the coin shining through the clear plastic evidence bag.

"Maybe the coin isn't a clue, just a coincidence," remarked Bill.

Phoebe smiled, "You know what I always say about coincidence—there's no such thing."

She couldn't help thinking that things were not looking up for Augusta, who had conveniently found the body and reported it. A coin was found under the body, so was there a struggle, an argument, maybe even a fight? The stamp indicated it was a coin from Augusta's mine. Though Augusta was acting remorseful, Phoebe wondered if it was actually guilt. She also remembered that Augusta was already drinking her never-before-noon Special Tea when she and the sheriff had arrived that morning.

Phoebe hated it when her mind went off on a tangent of *what if, what if, what if*—like Occam's razor. The more assumptions made, the further she felt from the solution.

Doc tagged along with the three to hear Augusta tell her story. He would work with the medical examiner to determine the cause of death, but he was anxious to hear what Augusta had to say. Lowering his voice as they stepped toward the UTV, Doc said to Phoebe, "I'll just listen so I can help the examiner."

Phoebe, nodding in agreement, told Joe and Bill, "Let me do the talking so we can keep it low-key and friendly-like."

The two men nodded, walked over to the UTV where Augusta was sitting, and stood close to the window to hear the exchange.

"Augusta, we need to hear how you happened to find Old Al. Would you be more comfortable talking here or should we all go back to the sheriff's office for some fresh coffee?" Phoebe's eyes never left Augusta's face. *What's really going on here?*

"I don't have much to say, so let's just get it over with here and now. What do you want to know?" Augusta said weakly, as though she was losing air like a balloon with a slow leak.

"Just tell me how you happened to come over to this mine and when. Do you mind if I turn on my phone to record what you say?"

"I don't mind, Phoebe. There's not a lot to say about Al. I got up early to come over and talk with him. You know, I'm camped for the summer over at the Last and about ready to move into town. Looks like an early winter and I don't want to get stuck up there. Has anyone seen what they say about it in the Old Farmer's Almanac?"

Phoebe shook her head.

Augusta continued, "So, anyway, like I was saying, I got up and drove the UTV over here, and there he was. Just like you see him. Facedown. Dead. I drove back down the trail to get a decent cell signal, called in to Roz to send the sheriff, and waited. Rose was over at my place, so I asked Hank to watch her."

"Who's Hank?"

"Hank's been working with Al all summer. He's the kid Al was training to prospect for gold. But he was treating the poor kid like a second mule and not teaching him anything, as I saw it. And Hank was feeling the same way, like it was a waste of his time."

"Where's Hank now, and does he have a last name, and was he here when you got here, and how did Rose get to your place?" Phoebe silently cursed herself. Interviewing 101 is just one question at a time, and there she was shooting off questions in such rapid succession that she almost lost track of what answers she was looking for. *Patience, patience,* she told herself.

Augusta caught her breath, "No, no, no. Hank was over at my place last night. He was headed into town to sleep in Old Paint. He's done with Al."

"Okay, Augusta. Why is he done with Al? And what is 'Old Paint'—a hotel or somethin'?"

"It's a long story," Augusta shifted on the vinyl seat. "You'll have to ask him. I just know Hank got tired of Al. He's a gullible kid, right? He wasn't learning how to prospect, just carrying all of Al's stuff. This is not what prospecting is about! I told him and told him, 'You better treat the kid right. You're not getting younger and you need his help.' But, no, Al had his way of thinking about Hank and kept saying, 'Ya gotta learn to walk before ya can run.' So, Al was making Hank do the grunt work for the prospecting. Oh sure, they found gold but Al didn't give

Hank any of it. The kid decided to quit Al and go to Oresville. At least the kid was smart enough to know better than to work for free."

Phoebe could barely take notes fast enough and was happy to be recording such a revealing conversation. "So, you came over here this morning, Augusta, but when did Rose show up at The Last Hurrah?"

"Al's idiot mule was there when I got up this morning!" Augusta's frustration with all the questions was starting to show.

But Phoebe had more to ask, "When did Hank get to The Last Hurrah? Did he bring Rose with him?"

"No," Augusta replied, as she thought back to Hank's arrival. "He hiked into camp by his lonesome around suppertime last night. He was planning to get to town before dark, find his car and sleep in it. I told him he could stay there at my mine while he sorts things out with Al. Some of my own summer workers left their gear and stuff before they headed back to their colleges two weeks ago. I always tell them that it'll be safe up here, but I did offer up to Hank that he could use what he needed."

"I thought he was going to sleep at Old Paint," Phoebe was starting to get confused.

"Old Paint *is* his car," Augusta clarified.

"Must be quite the car. So, how'd Rose get to The Last Hurrah if Hank didn't bring her?"

Augusta cracked a smile, "Mules are smart and she's been to my mine with Al lots of times. I always give her apples, and she's no dummy. Like a horse headed to the barn, she knows where the good treatment is." Augusta, pleased with her observation of Rose, let out a short giggle. "I guess I can keep her for a while, but I don't have any use for a mule. Where would I put her for the winter when I'm in town? I suppose there are laws about keeping a pet mule on the front lawn." She looked squarely at Sheriff Joe.

"Don't get me started, Augusta," Joe raised an eyebrow, tugged his ear, and looked away.

Doc spoke up, "Maybe we should call for the medical examiner to come up here." Everyone ignored his comment. No one wanted to spend more time on that abandoned mine site than necessary.

Frustrated with the litany of seemingly disconnected clues, Phoebe knew that putting together the story or a timeline of events was going to take some work. Interviewing Augusta was getting bogged down with irrelevant information. She needed a more formal discussion with Augusta. Standing next to a UTV on the side of a mountain, with a dead body nearby and three men who were listening but not making an iota of a difference, was not moving the investigation forward. *What's wrong with this picture?*

Phoebe turned back to Augusta, "Let's go talk with Hank, whaddya say?"

Augusta shrugged, "Fine by me. It's just past lunchtime. I skipped breakfast to get over here early. How about I put together some sandwiches and my Special Tea when we get over there?" Phoebe nodded, thinking she could take a hard pass on the Special Tea, but a sandwich would be great.

She tapped Doc on the shoulder, "Let's get the body loaded," then nodded to Bill, "We'll go over to The Last Hurrah to find this Hank character and have a little talk with him."

Sheriff Joe stepped away from the UTV and cleared his throat. "I have lots to get done back at the office, so I'll just ride back to town with Doc and leave all this to you and Bill. Let's get it figured out pronto. We need to know if we're dealing with a murder. If it's a murder, must have been someone Old Al knew. There's no sign of a fight, as I see it."

Doc nodded and stepped over to the body of Old Al, looked at Phoebe, and raised his eyebrows—*murder?* "If you say so, Joe."

Leaning one elbow on the open window's door, and watching for Augusta's reaction, Phoebe held up the evidence bag containing the gold coin, "By the way, Augusta, is this yours?"

Startled, Augusta reached to grab the evidence bag, caught herself, and quickly looked away at a distant stand of aspens. Dropping her hands in her lap, she went back to wringing the napkin and, with feigned innocence, asked, "Where'd you get that?"

POSSIBLE POSSIBILITIES

As everyone readied to remove Old Al's body from the Sunshine, Phoebe pulled her phone from her duty belt and snapped a few more pictures, for the record. Because the details of the taped-off crime scene had been altered by tire tracks and footprints made during their investigation, everything was photographed again.

The sun's heat was strong, though the strengthening wind made it feel cooler. Actually, it felt downright cold, morbid, making the fine hairs on the back of her neck stand up.

Something just felt off kilter. Maybe it was the change from "death by natural causes" to the possibility of something else. Sheriff Joe's comment, "If this is a murder . . ." had heightened her senses. Maybe it was how clean and undisturbed the area looked. If there had been a struggle, the dirt, grass, and weeds would not have appeared so pristine. *And what about that damn coin under the body and Augusta acting so funny about it?*

Old Al never went anywhere without his collection of prospecting gear, camping supplies, and Rose. *We know where Rose is, but where are his belongings?* He seemed one step away from homelessness, by choice, so he would never leave his gear behind. There he was in front of the Sunshine mine—dead, dressed for a Hawaiian summer, and without the accoutrements of his mountain life.

Phoebe had learned to trust her gut instincts. Some things just didn't add up, but she couldn't quite put her finger on the missing link. The initial assumption by all was death by natural causes because Old Al was, after all, old. The twist came when the sheriff suggested the possibility of foul play.

At first, Sheriff Joe had said that Old Al's death was "no big deal," as it was assuredly the result of a natural cause such as old age often provides. But, of course, any death is certainly a big deal to the deceased, as well as to those left behind. *Did Old Al have any family?* Phoebe knew he had acquaintances in town who might have more information about his story. She supposed she could ask Augusta. *Yeah, Augusta. Hmmm! How does she play into this if it is something other than death by natural causes?*

Deep in thought, Phoebe squinted her eyes and pressed her lips together. The vague feeling of unease annoyed her.

At the UTV, Phoebe and Augusta watched the men lift the body onto the combination carry board and transport stretcher and place it in the back of Doc's truck. Phoebe asked Bill to drive Augusta's vehicle over to The Last Hurrah. She and Augusta would ride in the sheriff's Wrangler.

Augusta insisted she was able to drive herself over to the mine, but Phoebe insisted, "This has been a long morning. Let's have Bill drive your machine and you can take it easy in the Wrangler."

When Phoebe and Joe had first arrived at the Sunshine that morning, Augusta looked to be sipping from a batch of her homemade Special Tea—a tea that had a way of dulling the senses, or so Phoebe had heard. Strong stuff that was reputed to be good for whatever was ailing the soul. Phoebe did not want another "accident" and knew that Augusta was in no state of mind to handle the rugged terrain.

Bill and Doc were long gone when Phoebe and Augusta took off in the Wrangler. The two women bounced and bumped back down the trail at a much faster pace than the ride up with Sheriff Joe at the wheel. The backside of the mountain had a more navigable trail, but the frontside trail had a shortcut over to Augusta's summer camp at The Last Hurrah.

Augusta's gaze followed the passing pines, admired the steep drop-off and neighboring mountainside, and fixated on a sky so blue it almost hurt the unshaded eyes. Phoebe, whose eyes were veiled behind her trademark green-rimmed, mirrored sunglasses, concentrated on the drive. Not wanting to influence Augusta in any way, she maintained the silence between them. She didn't want Augusta talking about the morning's events until the conversation could be recorded.

The first to arrive at The Last Hurrah, Bill called out to the young man sitting at the camp table, "Hey there. You must be Hank."

"Yup, that's me," said Hank. He slightly raised his hand as if to be called on and stood up to greet the uniformed visitor.

"I'm Bill Diamond. I'm the Undersheriff of Green County."

"What's up, Mr. Diamond? I was just killing time waiting for Augusta to get back."

"You can call me Bill. Augusta is on her way here with Deputy Korneal. She's okay, but I have some bad news to tell you. Old Al is dead. Augusta seems to be in shock."

As Bill spoke, he watched the young man's face and body language carefully for his reaction. At that point, the teen was a possible suspect in what could have been an unnatural death. Hank stood at the table for a moment, struggling to absorb what he had heard, and then seemed to sag into the table's bench.

"That's impossible! What do you mean Al's dead? I just saw him yesterday afternoon and he was fine. We were up at the Sunshine mine. When I left him, he was alive and well. I did wonder, though, why Rose showed up here alone this morning. Augusta did, too, so she went over to talk with Al about Rose and about how he treated me."

Just when Bill was going to ask about the way Al had treated the kid, Phoebe drove up with Augusta. Hank ran over to the Wrangler. "Augusta, what happened? What's going on? This guy just told me Al's dead. Is it true? How'd he die? Are you alright?" The kid was obviously upset, confused, and shocked.

"Slow down, Hank." Augusta planted her feet on her own mining ground, at last. "Let's all get over to the camp table and I'll get some sandwiches for lunch out of the Airstream. We could all use some food and drink. I'm sure I have some of my Special Tea all made up. Then we can talk about Al."

Augusta took pity on the kid. Food was always a good way to fill up space and would put off the inevitable talk. Augusta was back in control—they were on her turf now.

Phoebe came around the front of the vehicle and introduced herself to Hank. "Hi Hank. I'm Phoebe Korneal, Deputy Sheriff of Green County. You can call me Phoebe. I'm here, along with Bill, to meet you and hear about your experiences with Old Al."

She waited for his reply, watching him closely. Nothing. He looked at her as if he were trying to figure out what she had just said.

"C'mon, let's all sit down at the camp table and have a bite to eat," Phoebe directed, as she continued to scrutinize Hank for any sign of unease, nervous gestures, or rapid eye movement. *Not likely the kid would take off running, but one never knows with kids or guilty parties. Food first, and then a friendly chat with this kid and Augusta, too.*

Hauling people downtown to the office was not a great idea just yet. Phoebe could imagine Carrie Jean's face if she saw Augusta and Hank in handcuffs. Not a comforting image. She visualized a banner headline on Carrie Jean's High Country Gazette E-Blast! *Locals Guilty of Murder!* "Handcuffs" would suddenly be more than slightly exaggerated into a full-blown murder conviction, and headlines are tough to undo. An old Oresville miner once told Phoebe, "You can't talk yourself out of a problem you've behaved yourself into." Great advice to live by and apply to headlines written by her BFF, Carrie Jean.

The campsite Augusta had there at her mine was rough but functional. Her only luxury was the Airstream Classic, a top-of-the-line travel trailer she had purchased to summer in up at the mine. "Too many bears and mountain lions around for me to live in a tent," she often said.

The camp table sat eight people comfortably, yet she never needed all those seats. The kids Augusta hired for the summer usually ate on the fly and rushed to town for some fun. At one end of the table she had a metal storage box for plates, silverware, and whatever else was needed for meals. She kept a giant, heavy-duty Yeti cooler under the table for drinks. Milk was always stocked for the summer help, as she assumed growing kids needed it. Her Special Tea was off limits to the help, reserved for her, Al, and the occasional select guest. The local grocery store in Oresville had a standing order of supplies delivered each week to the site throughout the summer.

The rest of the camp held some seasoned but comfortable outdoor chairs. There was an expansive view of the lesser Rockies, a struggling stand of aspen trees to partially block the wind, and a rough ground cover of heavy-duty dark green sedum. Pine trees blanketed the neighboring mountains. There wasn't much else, except the fire ring and the big copper pot she used for everything, including washing her clothes. Augusta didn't need much. She loved summer life in the mountains and, of course, her time with Al.

Lunch was on the table in short order. Seemed like Augusta was feeling better once she had something to do and was back in charge. She called everyone to sit down, eat, and get to know her favored kid, Hank.

Rose was there and Al was not. Augusta was looking in control but not saying much of anything. Hank, on the other hand, was nervous and seemed confused. He was trying to piece together what little he had heard. No one had ever died in Hank's family while he was alive, so it was a new, unfamiliar feeling. He did not know what to do.

Phoebe and Bill were both very curious about Hank. From first take, he seemed like a nice kid, but definitely just a kid. Of course, as with all things, first impressions are not always the reality.

Phoebe took the lead. Her tone was easy and relaxed, like the gentle rays of the sun minus any wind. "So, Hank, how about you tell us your story—how did a young fellow like you end up in these mountains working with Old Al?"

Hank scanned the nature surrounding them, noting the irony—everywhere and nowhere to run.

MOVE IT ON OVER

Henry Klingfus, or "Hank" to most, was a mild mannered seventeen-going-on-thirteen with an extreme restlessness that gnawed at his friends who could only take him in small doses. He was a third-generation hippie. His parents were a by-product of Woodstock and the free-love era. Oddly, his mom loved country western music, especially Hank Williams, so her firstborn was named Hank. More formally, his birth certificate read Henry Williams Klingfus.

When his three siblings were born, his mom followed suit with the country western theme for names. George Jonas was a rendition of George Jones. Then there were two daughters in quick succession, Loretta Lin and Dolly Pardoné. Dad went along with the rather skewed interpretation of well-known country stars. Anything to keep peace in the family. How creative of his wonderful wife!

Growing up in Greenstone, Colorado, provided a quiet, unassuming life. Most kids his age agreed it was a boring, flat-lined town, except for the onslaught of tourists in the summer. The tourists provided cover or distractions so the town's teenagers could get away with almost anything. The authorities, business owners, and Chamber of Commerce enthusiasts were only focused on monthly sales tax revenue reports.

A town of a few thousand citizens, Greenstone had one recreational marijuana shop, commonly known as a "dispensary." There was only one of its kind in the entire county. The rest of the county was so conservative that the mention of recreational pot sent the county commissioners into coughing fits and furrowed brows to mask a greenish shade of envy—their cars having been spotted on many occasions in the Greenstoned Dispensary parking lot.

The recreational pot business was the personification of the goddess Hygeia, whose statue stood at the center of Greenstone and bore the inscription, "Health and wellness for all!" The tax revenues from the dispensary's sales were amazing, keeping the town council quietly giddy with the monthly proceeds.

The city fathers of neighboring Pikeview saw Greenstone as an enclave of weird old hippies who still had wooden pipes for their water system and no plan to upgrade the town's infrastructure. The current mayor of Greenstone, a retired-in-place lawyer, remained true to his motto "If it ain't broke, don't fix it." He went on to become a state legislator with that same motto as his campaign slogan. It was the same group of legislators who made John Denver's "Rocky Mountain High" the state's theme song.

Tourists meant zip to a kid of seventeen. In fact, the discussions among Hank and his friends were all about how bored they were and when they might leave their hometown forever. Hank was looking for excitement, independence, and mostly the peace of living without an annoying younger brother and two spoiled little sisters. Being the oldest of four kids was nerve-racking. Taking care of the sibs so Mom and Dad could work was not what he had in mind for a career path. Additionally, Hank was only five-foot-nine, and his younger brother was bearing down on his mark. Hank would likely grow taller, but for the time being, his status of "oldest, tallest, and in charge" was fading rapidly.

Like the rest of the flock of Greenstone teens, Hank couldn't wait to get out of that town . . . and so he did. At the end of his junior year of high school, he announced to his parents his decision to postpone his senior year. He called it an "Early Gap Year" and declared, "I'm headed to Oresville and I'll let you know how it goes."

Hank's decision was not a request. It was a fare-thee-well. His mom had suggested, "Let's take a run up to Oresville. You've never been there, and your brother and sisters would love a little getaway. We can all check it out!" His dad had ignored her suggestion, mumbling something about Hank being back when the snow flew in Oresville. He expected that to be in about August. Hank had shaken his head. It definitely wasn't going to be a family event. He was ready to be on his own.

Hank's parents had taught their kids to be independent thinkers, to make choices and stick with them. While his parents weren't thrilled about his decision to leave, Hank was adamant. For him, no further discussion was necessary. On the brighter side, his parents could turn his bedroom into a sanctum where they could escape, linger, perhaps even enjoy a cocktail without their children interrupting and demanding attention every other minute.

So, that was that. Hank would take the ancient Ford Pinto, a dog of a car referred to as "Old Paint." He stuffed his backpack with what he considered work clothes and added some camping basics he had scrounged from the family attic. He would go into the world to prospect for gold, fortune, and fame, minus family. With a working theory of "two birds with one stone," he could both get away from home and strike it rich. Flooring Old Paint, the determined young man tore up the Ute Pass highway, following the setting sun into his future.

Oresville in early June bustled with locals dressed in short sleeves and tourists bundled in jackets. Mining was going strong above the high mountain town. To the north hummed the immense molybdenum mine where Hank would seek a job, no matter how meager the wage. He would work as many hours as were needed to buy the equipment necessary to prospect for gold.

"Henry Williams Klingfus, Prospector." He sat up a little straighter in the driver's seat. It was a decent plan, shortsighted as it was for a kid striking out in life on his own.

To save every penny, he slept in Old Paint, curled up in the hatchback, like a pup on the dog bed his mom had given him. Cocooned in the sleeping bag he had pilfered from the family camping supplies, it became clear that the down mummy bag was actually a bit much for the summer nights at his base camp, which was wherever he could find to park overnight.

Like most Colorado mountain towns, Oresville was surrounded by National Forest land and land that belonged to the mining company. Over sixty-five percent of the state's forests were owned by the Federal Government. Hank figured one small piece of the forest land, owned by the People, would provide the perfect parking spot for him. He pulled Old Paint into a sheltered, isolated camp space that conveniently had a fire ring, and he settled in.

Just like camping, he said to himself. Accordingly, he sparked up a fire in the pit and opened a can of baked beans. His thoughts turned to finding a job, saving some money, and getting a decent place to live. *So far, so good,* he thought.

Following a cramped night's sleep in Old Paint, came a disappointing morning at Moly, the molybdenum mine. The employment office let Hank know that with no high school diploma there was no work for him there. Lounging in the Pinto, windows down, gazing at the awe-inspiring mountain scenery, he realized he needed a Plan B.

The trickle of the slow running stream nearby created a tranquil atmosphere in which Hank's thoughts could wander, though ever a reminder that record high temperatures and inadequate snowfall in the backcountry had the mountains advancing toward a severe drought. Like background noise, the stream continued in a lazy flow at a steady, uncompromising rate, similar to his stream of thoughts.

The sound of bells ringing and the clanking of metal on metal pulled Hank out of his reverie. Looking up the stream, he saw an old, rough-looking man trudging down the riverbed with a sturdy mule alongside him. The mule's bells and the old man's pots and pans made a helluva racket. Nothing and no one within a couple of hundred yards would be surprised by their approach.

"Hey there," called Hank to the odd duo.

The mule stopped to sip from the streambed as the old man strolled toward the Pinto. The man's whistling, if you could call it that, was more like a loud whisper of air through clenched teeth, but just as irritating as the real thing.

"Hey back at ya," said the old guy. "Name's Al. What's yours?"

"I'm Hank. Hank Klingfus." He reached his hand through the car window to shake Al's.

"What ya doing up here in the middle of nowhere's mountains?" the old man leaned closer.

"I'm gonna be a gold miner," Hank proudly announced. "Read lots of books about mining up here near Oresville, and I think there's lots of gold still to be had."

"Ever done any mining, Hank?"

"Nope. Haven't. But I've read lots about it."

"Well, reading and doing are two different things, son. And *doing* is the best way to learn. Been prospecting in these mountains for forty-some-odd years. Worked at the Moly for some of 'em. Me and my friend here, Rose, have learned a bit or two along the way. How long ya up here for?"

"As long as it takes to find my fortune." Such a dreamer he was.

"Where ya livin' then?"

"Right here in Old Paint." Hank tapped the side of his car.

Al was looking around at what little there was in Hank's rudimentary campsite. He quickly figured out the kid was on the edge of *not* living *anywhere*. Likewise, he was alone and he looked a bit lost, maybe even lonely.

Fortunately, he looked too young to be any kind of competition for gold prospecting.

"Hmm," pondered Al, "This might be a spur of the moment, but would ya consider working with me for the summer? I'll teach ya everything there is to know about prospectin' for gold, and you can help me and Rose haul all this equipment around the mountains."

Hank sized up Al and his mule, appeared to come to some conclusion, and eagerly replied, "You bet I would." *This could be my Plan B.*

"Okay then, Hank. Gather your belongin's and follow me on foot. The car can't come where we're goin'. Rose and me are headed to my campsite just below the Sunshine mine."

"On it!" Hank was already reaching in the hatchback for the dog bed mattress, sleeping bag, and backpack. "I'll take care of the car later. Let me just grab a few things here and I'm ready to go."

Quickly he locked up Old Paint and followed Al and Rose along the stream toward the forest of pines ascending the mountainside.

Prospecting was a solitary business, but Al was of an age where some young, strong lad could really help him out. Having someone to talk to was a plus. Al had learned from life that when opportunity presented itself, one must capitalize on it and talk with everyone or anyone. It hadn't taken him long to assess the young kid and figure he would serve as some good muscle and perhaps some good company.

So, off they went, Al, Rose, and Hank. Eventually, they angled away from the water and followed a rough trail up to a campsite that was set up just below the abandoned Sunshine mine.

"Here we are, young man. It's a transitory, makeshift camp, but'll do for us today." Al pointed a long, gnarly finger toward the tree line, "There's the Sunshine up there. Once a big producer of gold. I think there's still a good chance there's gold to be had there, but it'll require some work. You may have come along at just the right time. Put your stuff over there, next to the tent," Al waved his crooked finger again. "We'll get a shelter for you tonight. In the meanwhile, let's eat."

Hank was ready for some food, any food. He had the appetite of a seventeen-year-old and was getting tired of canned beans. The family meals back in Greenstone weren't so terrific, but there was usually some variety, never just beans from a can. Al had some venison that he roasted on his campfire while heating up some seasoned potatoes wrapped in foil. Hank thought he had died and gone to heaven. What luck!

While dinner was cooking, they worked on getting to know each other a bit. Actually, it was Al getting to know Hank a bit. Being a good listener, Al was adept at reading between the lines. When Hank whined, "Today was a real bust. I thought I was gonna get a job at the Moly mine easy peasy, but without a high school diploma I couldn't jump the first hurdle," it told Al all he needed to know.

Hank didn't see himself as a drop-out. Not yet, anyway. The mine employment office people didn't seem to understand his situation. It was his Early Gap Year, he had convinced himself.

Al had his doubts about the gap year bullshit, but was thinking, *the less said, the better.*

Dressed for a lifetime of prospecting, the old man's thick, denim coveralls were caked with dirt and spotted with patches. He gently kicked at the small pile of kindling with steel-toed boots. Admiring his heavy, long, black greatcoat and mad bomber fur-lined hat—perfect for the harsh mountain weather—Hank felt underdressed for his Plan B. Sitting there in jeans, a plaid cotton shirt with a button-down collar, tennis shoes, and a windbreaker jacket, he thought, *If I'm going to be a prospector, I need to get some clothes for this gig!*

Hank was mesmerized by Al's stories. The old guy was independent, free of responsibilities, and must have been making a living finding gold for the last forty-plus years. He was a prospector, through and through.

He had told Hank more than once over dinner, "I know the mountains, trails, and streams around Oresville like the back of my hand. In fact, we could say I know most of the Arkansas Valley. I've visited most areas a few times. Sometimes it's been good for gold, and sometimes good for a laugh!"

Hank didn't see any kind of topo map around. He also thought, despite the great stories, that Al looked more like a homeless guy than a successful gold miner. Of course, Hank didn't know what a successful prospector would look like. In fact, he wasn't really clear on what the difference was between looking successful and looking not so successful. Certainly, if Al had been at it for all those years, he must have been finding some gold. So, with a full belly and lots of great stories, Hank decided he was on the right track.

Looks like I found the perfect situation for the rest of the summer. I'll find a safe place to park Old Paint down in Oresville, and then I'll go to work with Al. Oh yeah, and maybe I'll take a few dollars I brought from home and hit the secondhand store, pick up some miner's clothes.

After Al cleaned up and banked the campfire for the night, he gave Hank a small lean-to to use for shelter. Grateful for the food and company, Hank settled down on the giant dog bed. His sleeping bag was perfect for summer nights close to tree line. He was feeling like a smile, safe and sound. His belly was full, there was an amazing blanket of stars overhead, wind steady in the high mountains, and high hopes abounded. With not much else to do once the sun hid behind the western mountains and the moon started to peak in the eastern sky, Hank sighed and fell sound asleep.

Today was my lucky day, Al thought as he made himself comfortable in his own tent. Some cheap—as in "free"—labor to help him through the summer. Augusta was always telling him he needed some help. Nothing permanent, but some seasonal help like she had—some college guys working for her mine just for the warm months. It was practical for her. She could take it easy, enjoy the sunny days, and watch the wildflowers bloom. Prospecting was a different way of mining from what Augusta was doing, but it sure was looking like Hank would fit the bill for Al.

HIDDEN AGENDAS

Sitting at Augusta's camp table, Phoebe asked Hank how he ended up working with Old Al. Bill and Augusta took a collective breath and held it, waiting for Hank's details.

Before the young man could answer, Phoebe raised a hand, "Wait a minute, I'll just record this, if you don't mind."

Hank nodded. Phoebe pulled her phone from the duty belt and told everyone she would review the conversation later, just in case. She hit the "record" button.

"Well, it just sorta happened," was Hank's reply to Phoebe's inquiry. "I just needed to get away from home and find my own way. Wasn't like my family was bad to me, it was just that I knew I needed to be out here in the mountains, prospecting for gold. Ya know, doin' somethin'. At home, I was just a glorified babysitter for my younger brother and sisters. It wasn't my deal, for sure. So, I came up here to Oresville to get a job at the Moly and learn about bein' a prospector.

"Anyway," Hank continued, "with no job, and a plan needing to be revised, I was sittin' in my car by this stream at what I called my Base Camp when I heard some banging and clanging. I looked up the creek, and there was this old guy trudging through the water. He was leading a mule loaded down with prospecting equipment, along with what looked to be everything he owned. He stopped to talk with me for a bit and introduced himself. Yup, it was Al. The next thing you know, he offered me a chance to work with him and learn about prospecting. All I had to do was some muscle work for him and listen. Are you kidding me? I jumped on his offer as quick as I could. So, he had me grab what I needed from Old Paint and follow him up to his campsite."

Phoebe was still stuck on the idea of a teenage kid living in a car. Was he homeless? Was he a runaway? What was his story? She decided to check on him later, but first things first.

"Ah, okay," Phoebe jotted some notes just in case the recorder didn't pick up every word, and to avoid staring holes through the poor kid. "By the way, how old are you, Hank?"

"I'll be eighteen in December."

Phoebe stored this special tidbit away for follow up and gave a slight nod to Bill.

Turning back to the young man, she smiled and asked, "And how did working with Old Al go for ya, Hank? I mean, how did he treat you? Did you learn lots about prospecting?"

She was trying to talk with him as in an easy, one-on-one conversation while Bill and Augusta listened. If Bill looked like he was going to jump into the interview, Phoebe would shoot him *the look*. They had all agreed to let her lead interviews when they first talked to Augusta at the Sunshine.

"It wasn't exactly like I thought it would be," Hank started out, somewhat bemused. "Seems like I did my part, hauling the equipment, loading and unloading Rose. I kept the campsite cleaned up. Used old branches from the pines to sweep the area, just like he expected of me."

Phoebe's pen raced across the notepad. *Swept the area clean with pine branches?*

Hank went on, "But Al, he just sorta kept his prospecting secrets to himself. Yeah, he gave me a tip or two along the way, but he pretty much just used me as his second mule. Ask Augusta. She knows what happened. She called me Al's sherpa."

Picking at her sandwich and sipping her Special Tea, Augusta had been only half listening to Hank and Phoebe. Hearing her name, she perked up and added, "And that's what the kid turned out to be, too. That's why I was going to Al's camp this morning. Was it really just this morning? Seems like this day is lasting forever. Anyway, after Hank came to The Last Hurrah yesterday afternoon and told me how Al was treating him, I decided I'd go see Al first thing next morning to tell him a thing or two. Meanwhile, I told Hank he could bunk here at my mine and use whatever he needed from the stash left by the summer helpers."

Hank cut in, "Yup, it went downhill from there. I'd had enough of Al and the way he treated me. At first, he was good company. He'd point out things I needed to look for that might mean there was gold around, and he told me great stories about his experiences in the mountains. But as time went on, he talked less and had me hauling his stuff more. And he never shared one flake of the gold we found.

"Every once in a while, he'd tell me he had some business to attend to and I should stay close to our campsite below the Sunshine to keep an eye on Rose. He told me to practice lookin' for clues that might lead to more gold. I did what I was told, but always wondered what 'business' he had to attend to in the mountains without me or Rose."

Phoebe thought for a moment and asked, "Hank, what happened yesterday? What made you come over to Augusta's place?"

"Well, it's a long story," Hank began, "and I'm not real proud of how it turned out."

Eyes widening, Phoebe gave Bill a sideways glance. They nodded to Hank and sat up to listen—all ears.

Hank went on, "Before Al returned from his 'business' trip yesterday morning, I'd pretty much decided I needed to stop carrying stuff around the mountains for him and try something else. I knew I didn't want to go back to Greenstone. And even though I haven't been to Oresville much this summer, I figured it's an okay town if I could find a job there. So, I made up my mind that as soon as Al got back, I'd tell him I'm done.

"When Al did get back to camp, he wasn't his usual self. He acted kinda distracted. I told him I'd be moving on and leaving first thing in the morning. He didn't say much to me. I thought he'd be upset, maybe even mad, but he wasn't. Then he told me it was still early in the day and maybe it would be best if I left right then instead of waiting till tomorrow. So, okay. No biggie.

"When I asked him for some pay for the work all summer or maybe even a share of the gold I helped him find, he told me if I wanted gold, then I'd better figure out what it takes to get it. He said, 'I'll share with you when I'm good and ready. And don't forget, I'm feedin' ya and givin' ya a place to live, all for free.'

"Free? No way! It made me really mad. I was working hard for him, and I wasn't getting a share of the gold? I just couldn't stand being with him one more minute.

So I told him I was heading out pronto before I said something I couldn't take back. He still wasn't yelling or anything. He acted like there was something else on his mind.

"I wasn't a happy camper and knew right then we were done. I grabbed my stuff and headed out. Walkin' the trail was tough goin', but it gave me time to think. I figured Augusta would understand, so I headed to The Last Hurrah to find her. She was always nice to me, and she knew Al better than anyone."

"Yes, I guess I do know him well," said Augusta with tears in her eyes. She couldn't bring herself to use past tense. "I just can't believe he's gone. We had a great run. I've burned through three loving husbands, yet Al's stuck with his wife for all these years. Through it all, thick and thin, we remained the best of friends."

"A wife!" Phoebe practically choked. "A wife? Who is she? Where is she? We need to notify her. A wife? This is the first I've heard of this." She shook her head and inquired of Augusta, "Where's she been? Oresville?"

Phoebe knew better than to ask this flurry of questions, but was so flabbergasted to discover that Old Al had a wife that she just couldn't help herself.

"Yes and no," Augusta answered. "They parted ways in Pikeville when they were young and hadn't been married too long. Al figured out the city life really didn't suit him, so he took off for higher ground. He got a job at the Moly to make ends meet, worked at placer gold mining part-time, and quit the Moly in 1997 after he found something more than a small bit of gold. I never asked him outright if he was married, divorced, or whatever.

"It appeared that their separation was more of a mutual understanding, as Al continued to supplement some of her financial needs. He held up his end of the bargain and made sure she got some of the money whenever he found some gold. I stayed out of it. Not my business how people decide to live—apart or not so much."

"Okay. So, what's her name and where is she now? Do you know?" Phoebe pried further.

"Her name is Martha, but she goes by Queennie," Augusta responded. "I think she still lives down the hill in Pikeview. I don't know anything else. Al rarely talked about her, but after a bit of overindulgence at the Club he'd sometimes mention her. I'm guessing she'd come up here to see him once in a while."

Wow, this whole situation is getting pretty tangled, thought Phoebe. *I need to step back and get a perspective on what's what. Meanwhile, I need Roz to find this Queennie-Martha's address for me so I can make a death notification visit tomorrow.*

Augusta added, "Just keep in mind, I'm not saying they were legally married or not. In fact, if you find out, I'd be interested in knowing."

Phoebe's gaze swept from Augusta to Hank, "Did Old Al ever mention a wife to you? Or did you possibly meet someone named Martha or Queennie in your travels with him this summer?"

Hank shook his head and mumbled, "Nope, just Rose, Al, and me."

"Okay then, thank you for your cooperation, Hank." Phoebe stopped the recording and flipped the notepad closed, "Bill, I think we need to get back to the station. I'll ask Roz to research the possibility of Old Al having a wife. Meanwhile, we need to review what we have so far."

Bill nodded, not taking his eyes off of Hank. Sagging in his seat, much like the Eeyore character right out of the Winnie-the-Pooh books, Hank appeared quietly disheartened.

Phoebe decided to try something else. "Let me just ask you one more question, Hank. Have you seen this before?" She pulled an evidence bag from her jacket pocket. It held the coin they found at the Sunshine under Old Al's body.

Hank reached out a hand to take hold of the small bag. He studied the coin inside. "Heavy. Maybe gold. It's stamped with "2014" so it must be pretty new. What is it?"

"I intend to find out," Phoebe assured him. "It's kind of rough looking, like a beginner's attempt to make a coin. Have you seen anything like it?"

Hank shook his head again, "It's stamped with "The Last Hurrah" on one side. Is it yours, Augusta?"

Augusta looked straight ahead as if she were on the other side of the mountain, and did not reply.

Phoebe waited a pregnant pause before taking the bag back from Hank. Stuffing it in her pocket, she stood up. They had heard all they could possibly stand for one day. *I need the autopsy report before I talk with these two anymore,* she thought.

Bill slapped both hands on the table and stood up. Nodding at Phoebe, he affirmed, "Okay then. Let's hit it." He, too, had gotten the drift that it was the end of any forthcoming information.

"I need to ask you two to stay here for now," Phoebe instructed Augusta and Hank.

"If you say so. I don't know what else to do," replied Augusta. Hank just nodded his head, still trying to grasp what was happening.

"I'll watch over the kid," Augusta volunteered. "He can help me clean up this place and maybe accidentally learn something about real mining."

"Good," said Phoebe. "One of us will be back tomorrow or give you a call to let you know what's going on. Augusta, you've got a short cell tower up here—if you think of anything you left out today, call the station and Roz will find me. Thanks for the talk, Hank. And, again to both of you, sorry for your loss."

Walking back to the Wrangler, Bill took the driver's seat. As he turned the vehicle around and headed down the mountain toward town, Phoebe felt grateful. She needed to think, not drive. Pulling out her cell phone, she called Roz. No answer. She decided to leave a detailed message rather than battle with cell signal the rest of the ride.

"Roz, we need you to do some research. It's possible that Old Al had a wife. There's a strong indication her name could be Martha, though she might be known around Pikeview as Queennie. Al's last name is Lewis, but that doesn't necessarily mean she used his last name. We're not even sure they were legally married. If you can find her, I need her current address and any other info you can dig up. If they were or still are married, I'll do the death notification tomorrow. Thanks. Bill and I are on our way back to the office. See you in a few."

Phoebe pocketed her phone, stared blankly out at the mountain range, and thought about the talk she'd just had with Augusta and Hank.

"There's more to this story than meets the eye, Bill," the detective mused. "Was Augusta somehow involved? Was the kid, Hank, part of this? Or was Old Al just sick? The kid did say Al was distracted and wasn't his usual self. Maybe it was just natural causes like we were first thinking. After all, Old Al was, well, old! It's the coin that's bothering me. What was it doing under his body, and where did it come from?"

"Right. Maybe we're not overthinking this," answered Bill.

ank watched as the sheriff's Wrangler pulled out of The Last Hurrah. He couldn't stop thinking about Al not paying him the money he was owed.

"Augusta, what can I do about the money Al owes me?" he asked.

The atmosphere darkened at the camp table. At first, he didn't think Augusta had heard him. So, he tried again.

"Any ideas on how to get the pay I earned or should I just forget it?"

"Let that be a lesson for you," Augusta chided the young man. "You went the whole summer without any pay, and now Al's dead so pretty much any hope of getting anything from him is dead, too." She did not want to talk about Al's gold.

Hank propped his head in a hand and scuffed at the dirt with his shoe. "But Al always seemed to find gold wherever we went, so I know he had *some* gold. After all these years, he probably had enough to last him a long while. There were times when he'd take off somewhere and leave me with Rose. I thought he just went to buy food for us, but maybe he put the gold in a bank in town?"

Augusta wrinkled her forehead, her patience running short. "There are more places to store gold than in a bank. If you'd lived around here and seen fortunes made and lost with stupid decisions, you'd understand."

That sounded rather vague and got Hank thinking. *Where's all the gold Al found? The coin the Deputy had was interesting, and I'd be willing to bet there is more than one of those somewhere.*

That made Hank wonder where Al spent his winters. He had told Hank it was too cold and there was way too much snow to stay at his campsite below the Sunshine all winter. Even Rose couldn't make it through the hundred inches or so of snow in most of the areas. The backcountry avalanches were too dangerous to do any gold prospecting.

Hank was speculating that maybe Al stayed with Augusta. After all, she had a place in Oresville and was Al's good friend. One way to find out was to ask her directly.

"Augusta, how did Al survive winters up here? Did he stay at his camp, or did he have a place in town or something?"

Augusta gave Hank the abridged version, "He stayed at my family's cabin. It's not much, but it's been in my family for over a hundred and fifty years. It's sturdy enough but needs work to keep the roof up and the walls intact. Suited him just fine, so he took care of it for me. It saved me from having to hire someone to fix it every year. He knew it was important to me for it not to fall to pieces and disappear. I don't know what I'll do with it now."

Hmmm, Hank pondered, *maybe Al didn't think banks were safe, so his gold might be stashed somewhere else.* Then he offered, "How about I go to the cabin and see if it's doing okay? I could maybe fix whatever needs fixin'.

Give me somethin' to do until I decide what's next." His offer of help might get him a pass to the family cabin where he could do a thorough search for Al's gold. "I could take Rose and get her out of your way, too."

Augusta thought it over, then rapping her knuckles on the table, announced, "Let's do it. You could go up there, take Rose, check it out, and snap some pictures. Spend the winter there if you want, but report back to me how it's standing and I'll see about how to preserve the property. Let me give you some money to tide you over. You're working for me now."

Augusta crunched the numbers in her head. The future of the cabin was murky. She would get her family lawyers to look at a land donation to the state of Colorado and a big tax break along with it. The family lawyers back in Omaha probably needed something to keep them busy since it had been a slow season of mining at The Last Hurrah. She could unload the cabin, help out the kid with a bit of work, and reap the rewards of a donation in time for the tax season. With Al gone, Augusta saw no reason to hang onto the property, or what was left of it anyway.

The Old Farmer's Almanac talked about snow coming late . . . *or did they predict an early start to winter this year?* Her memory was fuzzy. *Well, no matter, I'll figure it out later. Hank should be safe enough to go to the cabin now, make sure it's still standing, and I'll go from there.*

Augusta handed the extra cell phone she kept for the summer hires to Hank. "Charge it up. You can use it until you get on your feet. Text photos of the place when you get there. Tomorrow you and Rose can head out. I'll give you directions and enough food for a few days or so."

Hank's smile said it all. He felt the future looking considerably brighter.

WHAT DO WE HAVE HERE?

Phoebe and Bill arrived at the sheriff's office and walked past Roz with a nod of their collective heads. "Where's Joe? Any news on Old Al's wife?" asked Phoebe.

"Where's he always at in the late afternoon? In his office, counting down the minutes to quit for the day." Roz was in a surly mood. "As far as Old Al's wife goes, I don't have anything back yet. The feelers are out. I'll let you know in the morning. I'll be in early." Trying to look busy, she turned back to her duties to end the discussion.

Phoebe stepped into Sheriff Joe's office. "I need to update you on Old Al. Got a minute?"

Joe looked at his watch and nodded. "Make it fast. This is my night off. I'm waiting on Garcia. Whatcha got? Are we back to Old Al's demise being of natural causes, I hope?"

"Well, not exactly," Phoebe focused her detective brain to summarize it all for the sheriff. "The autopsy is the big factor here, but things don't exactly make sense. Bill and I went over to Augusta's mine and met the kid who worked with Old Al this summer. Old Al didn't exactly do right by him, and the kid got fed up and decided to move on. He ended up at Augusta's mine, and she took it upon herself to talk with Al about the kid's dilemma and straighten things out between them . . . except, as you know, when she got over to the Sunshine, she found Old Al up there, dead. Now we hear there's a possible wife for Old Al in the mix, which complicates things a bit. Know anything about that, Joe?"

"A wife? When did she happen?"

Phoebe took a seat. "Turns out he may have been married for all these years. We intend to figure out where she is, notify her, and get the details. Augusta thinks she's in Pikeview. I've asked Roz to look into it, but nothing yet."

Joe tugged his ear. "Alright then. I did call for the autopsy to be top priority, so we should have the report tomorrow morning. By then you'll have something to say to the theoretical wife." His eyes wandered to the clock on the wall and then to the door. No sign of Garcia yet.

Phoebe reminded him, "I'll need a few more days on the day shift. You'd better plan to cover my evening duty the rest of this week."

The sheriff again nodded and checked his watch. Phoebe took the hint and headed out the door.

Like synchronized swimmers, Bill came out of his office and joined Phoebe. Phoebe said, loud enough for Roz to hear, "We're going to the conference room so you can find us there if anyone asks."

"I doubt that'll happen," snapped Roz. "I'm almost done for the day."

Phoebe and Bill looked at her, then one another. *What's her deal?*

"I grabbed some paper. We can take notes," Bill waved his Bic pen in the air. "Let's see what we've got and stick to a high-level view. We don't have time to go off on a wild goose chase. I'm thinking death by natural causes, and we're done and outa here, good to go."

Phoebe stopped him right there. "We really can't assume natural causes without looking at all the facts." Feeling frustrated, she took a deep breath, suggested they take a short break, and stepped across the hall to refresh.

Located on the first floor of the Sheriff's Department in the Green County Office Building was a private back door that led to the sheriff's parking lot. The sheriff and deputies could slide in and out there without being seen or ambushed by uninvited visitors.

Office décor was Shabby Classic, not Shabby Chic. With little turnover, the office chairs looked comfortably personalized, and the desks were neatly organized. Everything was surrounded by a sea of standard issue light green walls. *The county probably bought this color by five-gallon buckets,* Phoebe often thought. Every room in the county building was drowning in the nauseating light green. Some designer forty years back had likely talked about the mentally soothing advantages of colors, having the same conversation around Harvest Gold and Avocado Green in the same decade.

The Guttural Green, as the county employees called it, was said to be soothing to one's soul for the nasty business of collecting taxes, holding court, and arguing with county leaders. It had also been a first-choice color for those in the submarine painting business, but the Navy had figured out that Eggshell White worked much better. Meanwhile, the county officials were still trying to deplete the earlier massive purchase of the green paint.

On top of the nauseating green everywhere, there was always a slight odor of burned coffee plus something else hanging in the air at nose level. Those odors wafted from the hallway where all employees could stand and drink coffee on their breaks while fanning the smoke from an illegal indoor cigarette.

The use of the hallway for breaks was the brainchild of a summer intern, whose only experience was a mail-order Master's Degree in Business. The same degree was likely used as bait to advertise the business school on the inside flap of a book of matches, back in the day.

Standing to drink coffee in a busy hallway turned a coffee break into a process and encouraged socialization, which was probably healthier than loitering in a chair at a table in an actual break room. An added benefit was saving the expense of using valuable office space for break space. The intern had calculated that it would save the county two and a half minutes per person per break, which translated to five minutes per day. Adding up to a mere twenty hours a year per employee, it increased overall productivity—a plus for the citizens of Green County.

The county commissioners were delighted with the out-of-the-box process improvement, and hired that clever summer intern as the county planner. Never mind he'd never had a job that included a break and, once he was hired, had never taken a break. He served in that position for twenty-six years, not once bothering to update productivity beyond what his slide rule had factored. At his early retirement party, he was given a coffee pot engraved with "Thank you and your slide rule for 26 years of service!" The party was held in the Break Hallway.

Regardless of all of that cost effectivity, the coffee pot was always on, albeit slightly scorched.

The locked back door kept out the nosey public. The exceptions were Jesús Garcia and Doc Watson, both of whom had the keycode for years. Sheriff Joe and Garcia usually played poker together one night a week while their wives met for dinner. The comforts of a small town included added predictability, week after week.

From the conference room, Phoebe and Bill could hear cowboy boots striking the vinyl flooring in the hallway. The sound came to a full stop as Garcia, in his usual black Stetson and bolo tie, hesitated at the conference room door.

"Hey, I was hoping to run into you two," the deep, husky voice of the Oresville native hummed. "How'd it come out at the Sunshine? Carrie Jean said this was likely a homicide. I believe she was thinking 'murder' in capital letters."

Phoebe's brain clicked at what Garcia was saying. "The last thing we need is a headline about *murder* in Green County, Jesús. Go with our first thought and call it natural causes. We called him Old Al because he was, well, after all, old. When we get the pieces put together, you'll be the first to know."

Bill tried to look busy, making no comment. It was Phoebe's deal, not his.

Garcia nodded to Phoebe and agreed, "Right. Anyway, I pulled Carrie Jean back from the ledge and asked her to settle down until the autopsy comes back. Next day or two we should have some decent information, correct?"

Phoebe affirmed, "That is correct."

Jesús Garcia was a high school buddy of Sheriff Joe's. Though two years behind him, they played together on the Oresville High football team, the Rockers. Just under six feet tall and supporting two-hundred-ten pounds of pure muscle, Garcia was a formidable defensive lineman the opposition dreaded to meet on the field. Thirty-plus years later, he still worked out every day. He loved to hunt and ski, and often tried to drag Sheriff Joe along, to no avail.

Garcia was like a wonderful uncle to Joe's four daughters. Godfather to each of them, he took his responsibility seriously. When he finally got married in his forties, he made it clear to his wife-to-be that the Jacksons were like family to him and a priority. The girls always listened to their Godfather's advice and, in turn, expected he would be at all their sporting events, camera ready. They were all older now and mostly on their own, but when they would visit, they still shrieked ecstatically at an unladylike pitch upon his arrival at their parents' house.

Having grown up in Oresville, Garcia stayed on to write for the local newspaper, the High Country Gazette. It was a great job for a kid fresh out of Oresville High, as he knew almost everything there was to know about every family in town. Three decades later, he still knew the townsfolk and their history. His ten years as Editor-in-Chief added authority to his experience, and his remarkable memory contributed delightful tidbits, innuendos, and overtones to articles, including those written by Carrie Jean, who was catching on fast. It helped that he had married a daughter of the richest family in the valley. The High Country Gazette had been in their family for nearly a hundred years. Some might say he was "retired in place."

"I'll just go find Joe and let you two get back to your whatever." With that, Garcia headed for Joe's office.

A long, narrow, well-worn table offered enough space for Bill and Phoebe to sit comfortably in the conference room and review what information they had. In a monotonic voice, Phoebe listed the facts, bits and pieces as they were.

Bill traded his pen and paper for a white board and marker, and took notes in bullet-point style. He exhaled, "From the looks of it, without an autopsy report yet, this still appears to be death by natural causes. Open and shut."

Bill separated the facts from his desire to be done and dusted. The list was short: a weird gold coin, the butt of a cigarillo, the way Old Al was dressed, no personal effects on him or anywhere around, and the Sunshine almost looked like someone had cleaned it up with a purpose.

Phoebe had to agree that the list didn't give them much to go on, and they needed the autopsy report before they could close the case. Otherwise, they had just out-there speculation and conjecture. She shook her head as if she were agreeing with herself and rambled on.

"We need to figure out this wife thing. Where has she been all these years? Are they really still married? Augusta didn't seem sure, either way. Maybe she's jealous that Old Al has been married all these years, and not to her. Married or not, though, I think it's kind of strange that Augusta seemed to know that Old Al gave this woman money, but she was pretty tight-lipped about the coin. I'm thinking this coin is hers, but where'd she get it? It looks new. Do you suppose she's making her own gold coins?"

Bill reminded her, "That would be illegal. Citizens can't make their own money, although, according to the sheriff, unique mine gold coins were made a hundred-and-some years ago when gold was first discovered. So, what's up with this coin dated last year and stamped with the name of Augusta's mine?" He added, "If the wife or whatever she is, is in Pikeview, maybe the PD there can do the notification. Save you a trip."

"I think not," Phoebe wasn't going to miss a trip to Pikeview to meet the mysterious Mrs. Old Al. "Roz used to live there and she might have some ideas about who's who and how they might help. Do you know anything about the town?"

"Not much," Bill replied, "It's a mixture of conservative military folks and young, outdoorsy types. Lotsa tourism and military supporting the local economy. We need to figure out first if she's even there."

"My thoughts exactly," Phoebe concurred. "Too late today to get the info. Roz said she'd have something for us in the morning. I should have asked the kid why Old Al was dressed up like he was. It was different, eh?"

Bill thought about it and rolled his eyes to the ceiling. Lightly whistling through his teeth, he announced, "Let's quit for the night. It's Burger Night at the Club. If we hurry, we can get a burger and hit happy hour 'Twofers'."

They stood, high-fived, and headed for the Club across the street.

BURGER NIGHT

Phoebe and Bill left the Green County Office Building and headed across the side street to the Elks Club. It had been a long day and they were exhausted. The sun, sinking behind the Massive, took with it the warmth of the day, trading it for a wind-chill of forty-five degrees. Thanks to the forest fire raging on the Western Slope and another in neighboring Utah, the sunset blazed. The ash and smoke in the air created a riot of color. Phoebe smiled at the Monet sky, happy to be doing what she really loved—wearing her detective hat.

With the end of the tourist season, patrol duty was easing back to normal. Though petty crimes spiked on payday, it was not a payday week, so patrol would be its usual mind-numbing routine. The move up to a detective assignment was only a temporary break, but it was a rare opportunity to prove her expertise to the sheriff and escape the tedium of patrol duty.

Sheriff Joe's lack of interest in Old Al's case was no surprise to Phoebe. Having been in the job long enough to have seen everything at one time or another, it took a lot to get him excited. He had an election coming up, and his skill was not so much in detective work but more at the "meet and greet" level. The only pizzazz in his flatline job was the occasional election, and the next one could be the final one before Joe's retirement. He and his Sweet M&M had recently been talking about that possibility.

Sweet Mary Margaret had started teaching when the girls hit middle school. It would be a few more years before she could retire. Her plan included Joe's retirement, a giant motorhome, and lots of travel at sea level, where she could teach online from the open road until she, herself, retired. She told "JJ"—her term of endearment for Joe— "Think of the money we could save on clothes if I teach online! No one would be able to see me. I could work in jeans and a halter top!" Joe had his doubts, but he had learned long ago to slowly nod and furrow his brow as if he were seriously considering what was being said.

Joe had his own ideas. He was focused on the coming election and many more years on the job. He saw himself in the Buns Up Bakery, shaking hands and greeting the neighbors he had known his whole life. He visualized sitting comfortably at the county leadership table during the commissioners' meetings and being quoted in the High Country Gazette by his life-long friend, Jesús Garcia.

After doing the good and noble job as Green County Sheriff all these years, why would I want to step out of the spotlight? Joe thought. *Why would I retire when the girls are grown and gone? Money isn't scarce . . . and after spending so many years with six of us in a two-bedroom, one bath bungalow that's now just the right size for us two lovebirds?*

In the end, he blew off the whole thought of retirement, nodded a final time to his Sweet M&M, and said, "Old Al's passing could be a straightforward strategy for my re-election without much effort."

Setting aside any further discussion regarding the subject of his retirement, Joe's Sweet M&M saw her plans vaporize before her eyes.

Bill and Phoebe were stepping off the curb mid-block—*jaywalking*—as a car accelerated around the corner. It would have hit her had Bill not grabbed her coat sleeve. Always interesting times in Oresville, with summer tourists trying to figure out where they were going, and always *going* at a higher speed than what was posted. No wonder speeding tickets were issued on an inflated basis during the short summer. So much so, the local paper highlighted the top offender with a "Speed Demon of the Week" listing along with the offender's name, their town of residence, and the speed listed on the ticket. By the time the weekly paper hit the newsstand, the offender had usually left town to return home. The little "Speed Demon" highlight was the first read for the locals, though only a nanosecond of fame for the offender. Jesús Garcia liked to inject into the High Country Gazette a sense of humor unsurpassed by the other papers in the river valley.

"Whoa, watch your step," Bill cautioned Phoebe. "Our health insurance doesn't cover you if you're breaking the law, ya know."

Phoebe did not comment on his unsolicited advice. An infrequent bit of 'rule breaking' like simple jaywalking didn't warrant handcuffs and prison time, but as Bill pulled her back to the safety of the curb, she was reminded of the reasons for even the smallest of rules.

Still not really paying attention as they walked, Phoebe's analytical mind couldn't leave the randomness of Old Al's death. First off, Old Al's demise was likely of natural causes. After all, he was, well, old. For the most part he lived outdoors except in the winter. But where did he hang out in the winter? God knows the winters above 10-5 were nothing passible, even if in a drought. It was still cold, regardless of snow depth or lack thereof. She doubted he went to Arizona or Florida for six months to enjoy the relaxing, warm climate. So many questions needing answers to determine whether or not his death was 'le cause naturelles'. And then there was the coin.

As Phoebe turned it over and around in her brain, she realized that Old Al's whereabouts in winter had never been questioned. She vowed to pay more attention to those citizens on the fringes of the county. That would not be too trying, as the population in the entire 350 square miles was a mere 7,500 or thereabouts. Factor another thousand or so residents who drifted in and out with the seasonal employment opportunities, and Green County was what would fall under the heading of sparsely populated.

Watching, paying attention, and knowing—all were important to her understanding the context of what made life tick there. She could do that without much effort. Already spending nearly seven hours most normal days in a sheriff's patrol vehicle insured such increased vigilance to be rather painless. Back in Salt Lake City, she had seen the same sections of town every day, month after month, and there was little excitement to break the routine. A small town like Oresville was another thing, as she had the run of the entire county—two thirds of which was national forest and not under her jurisdiction. She could definitely pay more attention to the *people* details.

Phoebe was glad to have Undersheriff Bill for a second opinion. He was a straight-up guy willing to work with anyone who was the lead on a case, regardless of age, gender, experience, or training. That applied, regardless of whether it was a traffic ticket or an investigation, such as that of Old Al's unexpected and, as yet, unexplained death.

Bill had pulled lots of patrol duty in Denver, but nothing by way of investigations or detective work.

Phoebe smiled a thoughtful smile. *This makes me The Lead (and only) Detective, along with being the Lead Patrol Officer. Moving here was a good thing!*

The Club was in a building built in the early 1990s. The building itself was considered new, as most of the other buildings on or near Main Street were built in the 1880s. Knowing the State Historical Fund had money to burn, the Town Council expressed interest in refurbishing the older buildings. The leadership of the fund was so dedicated and tight-fisted, the fund was referred to as the "Hysterical Fund" by those in the legislative branch. Whenever the state budget was running a shortfall, which was the normal state of affairs, the elected officials would eye the fund as a solution. "If only we could tap the Hysterical," was the usual grumbling.

Gambling funded the State Historical Fund, and with the economy booming, the gambling scene in Colorado was thriving. With its rich mining legacy and place in the state's history, Oresville was prime pickings for historical preservationists.

In 1876, Colorado had become a state without a capital. Though Oresville was one of several locations being considered for the future capital, the citizens and town leaders were not interested. Five years later, through popular election, Denver became the state capital.

There were so few women in Colorado at that time that the Women's Suffrage movement was considered to be no big deal by the male population. It was tough enough to even find a girlfriend or wife. With that in mind, supporting women's rights cast a favorable light on the men who were, in fact, always shopping. Colorado went on to become the first state that by *popular referendum* granted women the right to vote in 1893.

Though the Wyoming Territory had passed the Wyoming Suffrage Act giving women the right to vote years earlier, the two states' competition for the benefit of women was not so much about equality as it was about the free publicity to attract *more* women to the western territory.

The women who were born, raised, and stayed in Colorado were a narrow few in the 1800s. They were sturdy, tough-minded women, such as the women in Augusta's family who were well-known in Denver and throughout the state. Even with the right to vote, women were never included in the male leadership echelon. The leaders, both elected and not, called the shots from their offices in downtown Denver.

Historical photos of the City of Oresville and the early surrounding mining towns of Colorado were preserved on the walls of the Club, where many of the adult townsfolk stopped by at least once a week, if not daily. Willie Friedrich, most recent Exalted Ruler and perpetual manager of the Club, made sure the town's historical photos and portraits of the current leadership were always on display. In return, the leaders made it a point to frequent the Club, whether they were members or not. All were welcome—male, female, tourist, resident, elected leader. Membership would be addressed later. Willie offered free use of one of the two special event rooms for 12-Step meetings, as the profit margin on pop and coffee was big. Willie saw the Club as a support to the community. All the action was at the Club, where parking was plentiful, and friends and neighbors were usually gathered in the main bar.

It was Burger Night at the Club—burgers to fry on an outdoor grill, french fries to serve for an extra two bucks, and two-for-one drinks to pour. Willie's son, Brian, was pretty much the only bartender. He worked every day, and when business was slow, he doubled as the janitor. Burger Night was always busy, and Willie usually recruited his daughters, Jennifer and Ann, to take orders and serve customers. They helped their dad with the Club's accounting and did double duty on Burger Night.

Willie's partner of several decades, Rose Mary, set the standards for the kitchen, and it pretty much ran itself. Turnover in the kitchen was unheard of. Rose Mary appreciated the undivided loyalty of her kitchen help. All the free beer they could drink on Burger Night sealed the deal. The Club was built as a family business, and Willie made darn sure it would stay that way. Willie's motto "Family First" was embedded in the culture and radiated throughout the membership. Everyone was treated as family.

Smoking clouds of savory barbequed burgers advertised the summer Burger Night, tempting would-be diners all the way from Main Street. Who could resist a whiff of juicy burgers on the grill! A designated club member manned the grill—a rotational privilege that came with free beer. Tourists flocked to the Club as special guests. Of course, one had to show a member number to get the Happy Hour drink rates. Willie was nobody's fool.

When Phoebe buzzed in that night, she turned right into the bar hoping to run into Carrie Jean or Roz. Bill trailed behind but turned left to greet his friends in the dining room that overflowed with families gathered for the Burger Night special.

The whole place smelled of beer and french fries. The aroma of sizzling burgers wafted in whenever the side door opened. The kitchen crew, spare as it was, frantically fried up the hand-cut potatoes, constantly commenting about the need for new fryers and more of them.

The phone in the bar rang and rang until Brian picked it up, shouting over the noisy crowd, "We're havin' a great Burger Night at 10-5," followed by a pause as he looked around the room. "She's just walked in, hold on." He handed the phone to Phoebe, "Doc for you."

Carrie Jean, who was wiping up the last of her fries smothered in a ketchup-mayo mix, stopped a fry halfway to her opened mouth and looked over her shoulder at Phoebe, listening for her response. Phoebe continued a sideways wiggle onto the bar stool. Taking off her jacket and doing a head nod to Carrie Jean, she took the phone from Brian.

"Yeah, Doc, you just caught me." She listened for a moment, then added, "I'll be here for a bit if you want to drop the report at the office. I'll go back there after a burger." She listened for another full minute. "Okay, sounds good, I'll be there in an hour." Handing the phone back to Brian, she squared her bottom on the stool next to Carrie Jean.

Of course, Carrie Jean was all ears, "Long day and sounds like it's getting longer. What do we have on results, Phoebe?"

"Nothing at this point. The facts are still leaning toward a death by natural causes, so let's not speculate."

Brian read Phoebe's mind and offered, "One with fries and a beer, two up?"

"Better make it a diet something with the one and fries. Thanks, Brian."

Phoebe looked at Carrie Jean's attire. She dressed the same whether at work or lounging at home in jeans or leggings. That night she featured the typical t-shirt or two for the warmth of layers, her usual Rockies baseball cap, a ski jacket on the back of the bar stool, and canvas Tom's on her feet. By the end of each day, her wiry red ringlets popped out from under the cap and shone like each strand had its own lighting system.

"Well, what do ya think? Lotsa action for this little town, or just another day in paradise?" Carrie Jean was keeping her voice low. "I'm thinking *action*. It reads way too clean to be natural causes. What's up with how Old Al was dressed? All dressed up and nowhere to go?"

"I suppose a Hawaiian shirt is not so dressed up," chuckled Phoebe.

"No, but what gives with that shirt?" questioned Carrie Jean. "I've never seen him in anything except dirty, stiff-looking coveralls and a nasty old greatcoat. Then, this morning, he's sporting jeans with a wild shirt? A strange wardrobe accoutrement for a guy who is—or *was*—practically homeless and looked the part, if ya know what I mean."

Phoebe felt relieved that Carrie Jean was not there when Old Al's body was turned over. If the shirt and jeans seemed unusual to her, then the damned coin would be added to the flurry of questions. If Carrie Jean had been there and saw what they found, there would be no stopping her writing and speculation.

Phoebe looked directly into Carrie Jean's face, both of them raising their eyebrows. "Let's just keep it on the back burner for now. It is what it is, right?" she said, feeling the need to steer Carrie Jean in another direction before anyone else overheard and started adding more questions—questions for which she had no answers.

Chugging her diet pop too fast, Phoebe belched in an unladylike fashion. Amid the noise of glasses clinking and people talking, no one seemed to notice. What her stomach *really* yearned for was food. At last, her burger appeared with the fries still sizzling.

The Club made their own freshly cut fries—lightly peeled and waiting in a water bath, each one slammed through the potato cutter and dropped into an available fryer to sputter and pop to perfection, fulfilling the immediate order. Willie had worked at a fast-food joint in the early days before frozen everything from headquarters became the corporate *process improvement* mandate. He remembered the crisp, fresh fries from the three or four overnight water baths that removed the excess starch. Those fries never stuck together. Removing the excess starch was the key to a crisp fry, and Willie was living the dream. So were his happy customers.

Sitting at the bar, Carrie Jean and Phoebe enjoyed their meals while chatting. Comfortably snug in state-of-the-art washed denims, Born boots, and a red buffalo plaid Orvis flannel shirt over a shocking pink tank, Roz made a grand entrance and took a seat on the other side of Carrie Jean, making sure that Brian would have an eyeful of her voluptuous breasts trying to escape their captivity.

Leaning over the bar, she motioned to Brian and, with her sultry Cajun accent, drawled, "The special, double the fries, and a two-up on a Sazerac." Smiling scarlet red lips made it clear that Roz was ready for a fun Burger Night at the Club.

Being from the bayous surrounding New Orleans, Roz never missed a beat to celebrate her birthplace with that special drink versus her adopted state's craft beers. Colorado's over-abundance of unique craft beers was infamous. If one had a garden for growing hops and a decent stove, another craft micro-beer was born.

The truth be known, Roz never drank Sazerac when she lived in Louisiana, because she was not old enough to drink. She had worked hard through high school, selling magazine subscriptions and Avon products with a focus on getting out of Louisiana. Her goal after graduation was to move to the highest town in the nation from the low, wetlands of the Louisiana bayous. Her plan had been solid and even studied, but the Greyhound bus ride ended in downtown Pikeview, Colorado, a hundred miles short of Oresville. As she stepped off the bus with just a duffel bag and enough money for a few weeks, her first thought was a decent meal. Her second thought was a long, hot shower, and the third was all about a job. There was no easy way to Oresville and she knew from experience hitch-hiking was not a safe choice.

Next door to the Pikeview bus station, there was a mom'n'pop diner known as The Bus Stop Café. It was there her plan abruptly took a detour. The place was swamped. A "Help Wanted" sign was prominently displayed in the window. Roz went in, mentioned the sign, and was immediately put to work busing tables. Pop called from the kitchen, "We're closed. Breakfast is officially over." She was interviewed right then and there by Mom. The job of waitress included free rent of a small efficiency room above the café in place of an hourly wage, along with keeping any and all tips she earned.

The café was a popular and quirky breakfast spot with the locals. When they ran out of eggs and green chili, they shut the doors each day. The same business model had been in use for over thirty years, and the locals were never upset when they arrived too late for breakfast, whether it be eight in the morning or two in the afternoon.

The downtown location was ideal for meeting people and dispelled the need for a car. A tall, slim Louisiana beauty with shiny black hair, dark eyes, and bright red lipstick, such as herself, would have no trouble making new friends. Zydeco music and her Cajun accent made Roz and the café worth standing in line for. She met more than a fair share of fellow millennials within the first week.

After a few years in the food business, a busy nightlife in downtown Pikeview, and a disappointing romance, Roz answered an online ad for a position at the sheriff's office in Oresville. She was trained in worthless shorthand and typing (useless in Colorado, she came to discover), but her saving grace was that she was a wizard when it came to people skills. Roz could talk the talk. At twenty-three years old, she headed to Oresville for a fresh start with the Green County Sheriff's Department, and her goal of living high was achieved.

Roz pulled cash from her jeans' front pocket, her cell phone from the back pocket, and put both on the bar. Quoting from the Old Farmer's Almanac, she quipped, "Guess winter's back, and I had to work the weekend we had summer!" Hearing that, the regulars seated at the bar chuckled good-naturedly. Just a "weekend" of summer, regardless of what month a calendar called out, was always a fun mention.

Roz was actually quoting a friend of hers, DeDe Williams. DeDe had grown up in Climax, Colorado, a town that was literally relocated to Oresville in the early 1960s. That move made her both a transplant and a native of the area. DeDe could talk about the town's history faster and longer than anyone. She never missed an opportunity to comment on the mindless decisions made by engineers who were constantly in search of molybdenum. DeDe's favorite example was how the *entire* town of Climax was moved off a mountain so mining for moly could go open-pit. Though nearly sixty years back, the memories were vivid. An exemplary story of "anything for success," as it brought full employment for the town. The story always elicited the shake of a few heads and general comments of full agreement about how business success trumps concerns of the lowly citizens every time.

Roz looked past Carrie Jean to Phoebe and, keeping her voice low, asked the obvious question, "Well, when are y'all gonna arrest Augusta?"

The business they were in precluded any of those at the bar asking the same question, even though the news of the passing of Old Al had spread like the proverbial forest fire swept by the winds of something new to talk about.

It was, indeed, the trigger that shot Carrie Jean into the bright, beckoning land of opinion. She felt compelled to protect her friend, Augusta, by stating, "Old Al's trainee is the logical suspect here. After all, the kid was with him all the time and Augusta said they had a falling out yesterday. My money is on the kid. Besides, Augusta would never do any harm to a business partner like Old Al."

"Partner? Why would you call Old Al a partner with Augusta?" Phoebe questioned, using her nonchalant monotone to camouflage her surprise.

Roz piped up with her own opinion and logic, "I'll tell ya, sister. They've been in business or some kind of partnership for years. Nothin' formal with Augusta's lawyers and such. More of a handshake, which would meet the needs of a gold hunter. If you were Old Al, what would you do with your gold? Assumin' you found any gold, right? Would he stop by the only bank in town and ask them to convert his gold to cash? No way!"

Roz lifted the first of her twofer Sazerac drinks just high enough to see the bar's neon lights reflected in the glass. "Prost, Mary," she whispered and carefully took a lingering sip. "Whew, Brian, I think you nailed it on this one!" Her eyes watered as she slowly stirred the drink with the orange peel.

Through her short days of work back at the café in Pikeview, Roz had met a regular patron, Mary Henson, who became a dear friend. Mary had been on a historical guided tour of the New Orleans area with the local Fine Arts Center, where she had made many great discoveries—and Sazerac was one of them. Mary shared her discovery and its unique history with Roz on Roz's twenty-first birthday. It became the Designated Roz Drink. A stiff drink as New Orleans cocktails go, blending expensive ingredients, such as Absinthe, bitters, Rye whiskey, and Cognac, it was the best deal in the house during Happy Hour at the Club. Roz always saluted her buddy, Mary, every time she took the first sip.

Lowering her voice another notch, Carrie Jean spoke in a conspiratorial tone, "No way would Augusta be in a real business with Old Al. She felt sorry for him scratching out a living one little speck of gold color at a time. The search for color is, or was, like an obsession with him. He comes from Pikeview and worked for years at the Moly as an engineer, prospecting on the weekends. He quit his job there something like ten or twenty years ago when he found one lousy nugget. Just like that, he gave up his real job to tramp around the mountains, wade in the streams, and prospect for gold. I even heard his old job had great pay and benefits."

Carrie Jean continued her debate-argument, "She lets him stay free at her cabin for the winters. Oops, meant to say she *used* to let him stay in her family cabin. Can't get used to using past tense with Old Al. He didn't have any other options for winter, and Augusta needed someone to look after the original family place. Match made in heaven. From what Augusta told me when I talked with her at the Sunshine, I believe her. That leaves the kid as the primary person of interest." She gave her old friend, Phoebe, the strong, steady *look*—the kind of look only BFFs can instantly read—and her eyes stayed on Phoebe to see if she got the message.

Phoebe met her gaze, and then turned to Roz who nodded her head in agreement with Carrie Jean. Phoebe's mind percolated. *What's this about Augusta's cabin? How did they know, and why have I never heard this?*

"Geez. Where is this cabin?" Phoebe asked, continuing with calm composure. "Must be quite the cabin if he could spend winters there. How does a mule fair in deep snow at thirty-six below temps? Or did he leave Rose elsewhere?"

Roz spoke first, "I'll tell ya, sister. It's not too far from the Last, as I understand it. Augusta has talked about it, but I've never been there. I understand it's partly furnished with a cook stove, a bed I suppose, and an outhouse. The usual. It's a miner's cabin. Not much to write home about, I'll tell ya. I have no idea what he did with Rose. Mules aren't really pets, are they? Who knows how men think about mules? Most of today's miners around here have a dog at most, as I see it. But a mule? God knows." She crossed her eyes, pursed her lips, and cranked up her eyebrows, clearly sharing her message regarding pets and men. Brian made busy trying not to respond to their line of talk.

Carrie Jean nodded her head. She and Augusta were friends, but she had never been to Augusta's family homestead either. She didn't want to say anything that would support the theory Roz had about Augusta. Carrie Jean knew Augusta well enough to see how devastated she was that morning. In her experience, Augusta had never looked so sad, nor said so little. Augusta was usually the one to do most of the talking, animated even, but not that morning.

Carrie Jean's eyes widened. *Then again, maybe something had happened between Augusta and Old Al, and now he's dead? No way. It's gotta be something with the kid he was training. On the other hand, and I hate to even think about it, all of Augusta's husbands have died,* she thought, suddenly feeling a little shudder run through her bones.

Phoebe made a mental note to talk to Augusta about where the cabin was located. *I'll go there and check it out,* she thought. *I need a better feel for Old Al and a clearer picture of what his life was about.*

She decided to take a chance and questioned Carrie Jean further, "I understand Old Al might have had a wife somewhere. Did you ever hear about this, or maybe meet her?"

Carrie Jean shrugged her shoulders and shook her head. "News to me," she quipped.

Phoebe decided she had shared enough with those two and dared not mention any more about the wife or the coin at that point. Though she thought the world of her friend, Carrie Jean could be a loose cannon when it came to details and conjecture—dangerous even. Roz would get the details at work, and that would help her fill in the blanks. For the moment, she would call a lid.

"I need to get some work done tonight. Can you two excuse me? Maybe I'll see you tomorrow. Please try to keep any thoughts to yourselves, and call me if *anything* occurs to you."

With that, Phoebe unfolded her five-foot-ten-inch frame from the bar stool, put on her jacket, adjusted her thirty-pound duty belt, and as inconspicuously as possible, tried to shift her shirt under the bullet-proof vest. She went in search of Bill to tell him she was headed back to the office.

Bill was sitting with friends and their families at a big table. He was eyeing his hamburger. Well into his craft beer twofer, he looked to be settled in for the evening. Bill had lived in Oresville a bit longer than Phoebe and had established a comfortable social life. The mining town culture seemed to fit his personality. He missed his kids, but his friends' kids made up for his own. And they were better behaved than his "city kids." His ex-wife was another matter. Just that year, he had established proof that she earned more than he did. That meant he no longer had to pay her spousal support, and they would split the cost of raising their kids 50-50. Additionally, with the extra bucks, he could double up on the fries at Burger Night without a second thought. Life was good at 10-5 for Bill.

As Phoebe entered the dining room, Bill stood to greet her.

"Kind of early to be leaving, isn't it? What've ya got?" he asked quietly, as it seemed the entire room had taken a collective breath that rested at the top of an exhale.

Phoebe, practically whispering, gave him the news, "Doc called. The autopsy report is almost ready and should be over at the office. I'm headed there now. I'll take a peek, confirm it's as we think, and head on home."

Patting his hair to be sure it was all in place, and without listening to what she was saying, Bill continued, "This is the big talk in town. Maybe we should arrest someone. If nothing else, just for questioning. We'd probably look more on top of it, ya know? Mind you, I'm not calling it a crime. The sheriff is up for re-election. Appearances count in times like this."

Trying to act casual, Phoebe turned her gaze toward the coffee station. Wrinkling her nose and lowering her voice to a whisper, she replied, "I don't know who we'd arrest. Augusta? She doesn't look the type. This kid, Hank? He looks more like a deer in the headlights, not a guilty party. Besides, how would an arrest look when we are assuming natural causes? No, we'll wait and see what the report says and use investigative details to go from there. I need to follow protocol here and get the wife notified—if there *is* a wife to be notified—before we charge off on random arrests. Just cool it. Enjoy your Specials and I'll take care of it."

Bill nodded, patted his forehead with his paper napkin, and looked greatly relieved or at least, reassured. He didn't actually breathe a sigh of relief, but the forehead pat sent the message.

"Alrighty then, Deputy, thank you for your service. Good night," he said in a voice that could be heard by friends and others at nearby tables.

With all eyes on him, Bill sat back down. With that, the room filled with air on the collective exhale and Burger Night dining resumed.

Phoebe had already turned and stepped toward the door. She had more on her mind than public appearances. The autopsy report was ready.

AWE-TOPSY

Phoebe entered the sheriff's office. "Hey there, Markie," she quipped, "Quiet night?" Mark was the deputy on desk duty for the night. "Markie" was his cop shop nickname. It was tradition, and Oresville deputies carried a singular moniker at the station house. Over the years, those monikers had become a way of building comradery and unique acceptance for Oresville's small cluster of law enforcement. The nicknames, however complimentary or otherwise, stuck with the officers through their career, or at least as long as they could stand living at an altitude of 10-5.

"So far, so good, Fifi. The autopsy report is back there on your desk. Hope it's good news and the death of Al can be put to rest."

"Me too." Phoebe couldn't have agreed more. "There's lotsa theories about his death, and I'm hopin' this report will put it to bed. Fingers crossed, anyway."

She headed down the hall to the bullpen she shared with the rest of the force. She wasn't thrilled with her nickname, but trying to protest or suggest an upgrade would not work. Instead, it would likely increase the use of it. So far, the rest of the deputies used it, but not Bill or Sheriff Joe. To Phoebe, "Fifi" was a carryover from her work in Salt Lake City. She couldn't shake it. She wondered who had researched her history and been told about the Fifi bit.

There was a TuTu's Washateria in Oresville, and Phoebe thought her nickname and that place of business sounded somehow related. More than just a coin operated laundry, the owner, TuTu, believed calling it a "washateria" encompassed a broader spectrum of service. As a bonus, TuTu served Bloody Marys with a homemade breakfast every morning. Despite the imagined similarities between their names, Phoebe needed to let it go.

Once at her desk, she looked at the sealed envelope. "Please make this death be by just natural causes," she whispered as she mentally said a little prayer for what she hoped to see. Taking a deep breath, she slid her fingernail under the envelope's flap, opened it, and took out the report.

The first thing she saw was the heading "Preliminary Report." Reading on, she got her answer. When the medical examiner did the autopsy on Old Al, she had apparently found some questionable results and decided a more in-depth analysis needed to be done. Having observed the entire procedure, Doc concurred. So, although Phoebe received *some* information, the final result was yet to come.

The report estimated the Time of Death was approximately two to three hours before Doc Watson had arrived on the scene, and stated the Cause of Death was as yet unknown, listing a bruise to the left kidney and discoloration of the skin as items requiring further analysis. A hematoma was observed on the corpse's back, near the kidney, yet the bruise could not have been a fatal blow. There were indications of other factors impacting his death that would require additional study, including a toxicology report.

Next was the critical discovery. Old Al's internal organs had deterioration consistent with long-term arsenic poisoning. His skin had remarkable indicators—multiple skin lesions and rough, swollen areas of the skin on various locations of the body, and his fingernails had the telltale white streaks. The tox report would confirm Doc and the medical examiner's suspicions.

"Arsenic poisoning!" gasped Phoebe. "What the hell is this all about?"

The report went on to say that it appeared Old Al did not get one big dose, which would have killed him on the spot, but that he had consumed small amounts of arsenic over time, compromising his whole system. The report also stated that the stomach contents were non-existent, indicating he had been vomiting—evident in his throat and mouth particles. Ingested over time, arsenic would have induced slow, gradual organ failure. But was it the organ failure that killed him? Hence the need to do a lab analysis to confirm arsenic as the actual cause of his demise and rule out any other plausible causes.

"Well, isn't this just great," mumbled Phoebe. "Arsenic poisoning, a punch to the back, and a single gold coin under his body. Lots of clues and I'm clueless. What or who struck Old Al? Did someone actually hit him or did he walk too close to a tree and get hit by a swinging branch? And how would he have been slowly poisoned with arsenic? Where would he have been exposed so regularly? Then there's the pesky coin. How did it get under his body? Didn't the kid say that Old Al was acting as if he were distracted and not himself yesterday afternoon? I thought Old Al was just upset about parting ways with the kid, but maybe he felt sick and couldn't wait to get the kid out of the way. I thought this autopsy report would clear things up, yet it appears to have only darkened the waters." The walls she had been talking to did not respond.

Having nothing more to do at the office, and exhausted from the long day, Phoebe decided to head home.

She would contact Bill in the morning and bring him up to speed on the report as she drove to Pikeview. What would she tell Old Al's wife, or ex-wife? She had nothing definitive based on the preliminary report, but she still needed to visit the theoretical wife to report his death.

"G'night, Markie."

"Take care going home, Fifi," Markie replied. "Missed having you on patrol this evening."

"Hope to have this situation wrapped up soon and be back to normal again. Nothing like the old routine to keep us all comfy. Meanwhile, I'm headed to Pikeview first thing in the morning. I'll leave my truck in the lot and drive a patrol vehicle home. Don't let some ambitious person have it towed," she tried to laugh.

While Phoebe acted like all was well, inside she was tense. Was the natural cause of death really a homicide, albeit a slow one? *How does the gold coin figure into the death? What's the deal with the bruise on his back?* For the umpteenth time in one day, she was mulling over Old Al's passing and the autopsy report. It had all become way too complex. So much to think about. But then, complex was right up her alley. She loved detective work and reveled in the opportunity to do her thing.

I'll get a good night's sleep and head out in the morning. The drive will give me lots of time to think about what we know so far and put two and two together.

Pulling into her parking spot at the rented trailer, Phoebe sighed in relief. Stepping out of her patrol SUV into the cold, the still night air nipped at her face and hurried her toward the door. Once inside the singlewide, and thoroughly exhausted from a long Day One of Old Al's passing, she headed straight for the bedroom. The cool, stale air from being closed up all day mirrored her state of mind.

Locking up the Glock, Phoebe plugged in the cell to charge and carefully placed the thirty-pound duty belt on the dresser. Promptly shedding her many layers of clothes, she draped the heavy vest on the back of a chair and hopped into a hot, relaxing shower—as relaxing as it could be while battling the nagging feeling of missing something important regarding Old Al. The steaming hot water eased her tense muscles. Twenty minutes later, dressed in her warmest granny gown, she set the alarm for early morning and climbed into bed.

Tomorrow will be a new day that will, hopefully, bring new insights into the situation with Old Al. If I can find this Martha Somebody in Pikeview, maybe I can get some much-needed understanding. Maybe the coroner will have some news from the pathology work sooner than later. And, if I stop by Greenstone on the way, maybe I can get some more details on Old Al's sherpa, Hank. Maybe, maybe, maybe. With that final thought, Phoebe's eyes slammed shut.

INFO-MINING

The alarm went off way too soon, signaling Day Two of Old Al's death. Phoebe had been awake for several hours and the alarm was just an afterthought. She had created and run through a mental *to-do* list first thing that morning, reviewing and adding to her list many times.

The night before, Phoebe had left a note for Roz reminding her to get Old Al's alleged wife's address, maybe a last name, and a phone number. She also hoped for the woman's place of work, if she could be so lucky. She knew that Roz would access the state records and county land records, and that could add to the picture of Old Al's life.

Practically erupting with questions, Phoebe sighed. *Did Old Al have a history other than Oresville? Then the kid, Hank? Is he a situation in all of this? The arsenic poisoning, where would it have come from? Am I making a mountain out of a molehill in my usual overly active suspicious brain?*

Not 100% arsenic as the cause of death at this point, but the tests will confirm one way or the other. According to Doc, the probability is more along the lines of long-term exposure to arsenic than a one-shot deal. Old Al picked up this sherpa the first of the summer, about two months ago, so the kid would not have been a part of this. Where would a placer miner pick up arsenic? When it comes to random acts of violence, impressions don't weigh on the scales of justice. The cut-off age for Juvenile law is sixteen years old. In the eyes of the law, Hank is an adult, albeit a young seventeen.

The way Phoebe's mind worked, she could not let go of the details. They built and churned, and then paused for a fraction and built some more. She admitted it was a grinding process. "Let me grind on this," she would say, even when off duty. She was adding more pieces to the notion of Old Al's demise via natural causes, as they unfolded from the beginning. With the final autopsy lab results a day or so away, the space was there to build the story, the details, and the context of what had gone on. Her instinct was that his death was not by just natural causes.

Something unknown had happened at the Sunshine, and Phoebe could never ignore her tried-and-true gut feelings. Her plan was straightforward—head to Pikeview to find the wife, or ex-wife, and stop in Greenstone on the way in order to get some insight into the kid, then be back home in time for the late-night Denver news at ten. It would be a good day. Done, done, and done.

Driving with cell service at three bars, a twenty-ounce Yeti Rambler of hot, black coffee in the cup holder, and the sun up on another day in the Rockies, Phoebe's patrol SUV crested Trout Creek Pass. Not one other car, truck, or otherwise, in sight. As the majestic view of South Park came up, she marveled at how flat the entire area was between the Breckenridge skiing mountains to the north, Wilkerson Pass to the east, and Buffalo Peaks to the west.

She called into the office on the private line and Roz grabbed the phone before the first ring had cycled.

An early six-thirty but Roz was already at her desk. She answered with the usual, "Good Morning, we're having a great day at the Green County Sheriff's Office. Rosalind Marie Boudreaux speaking."

"Roz, you could see it was me calling on the caller ID. Do you answer your phone like this when it rings at home?"

Roz ignored the question, laughing, "I knew you'd call for help at the butt crack of dawn."

"Yeah, yeah, I hate it when you're right," Phoebe smiled into her smartphone. "Find anything? I'm headed to

Pikeview right now. Planning to stop in Greenstone on the way."

Roz clipped her off there, "I already heard from our head honcho and he says you can skip the car ride and stay here until more information comes in on Old Al. No sense in running off on a wild goose chase. He must've talked with Doc."

"Well, pretend you never heard from me and that fixes the car ride advice, regardless of his cautious, typical sheriff's thinking. What's going to happen at the office today? I'll tell ya—nothing. Take it slow and easy? Drag it out for the rest of the week? Next week? Next month, even? Nope, that's not how I roll, so you can keep this little tidbit to yourself. Just forget you heard from me."

Roz let out a chortle and played along with the conspiracy, "Who did you say you were?"

Phoebe snickered in cahoots. "I'm headed to Greenstone as we speak. Already over Trout Creek Pass. I'll check out this kid, Hank—family, school, friends, whatever. Supposedly, he is, or was, a high schooler there and now taking what he calls an Early Gap Year. What kind of crap is this? Is he a dropout? Where are his parents anyway? I'll stop by the school and see what they can share with me, get more of a feel for him and his family."

Roz was sipping her Union brand of chicory coffee. She was practically raised on Union coffee, which, in the digital age, could be ordered online and delivered to her in Oresville. No need to stock up when she'd go to Louisiana for her yearly visit to her "mawmaw"—the Cajun name for grandmas. The chicory coffee helped start each day with the taste of home, and she thought chicory was good for one's liver, especially after a long night of overindulgence at the Club.

Roz added, "You know I lived in Pikeview, next door city to little ol' Greenstone. A good friend of mine back in the day is now the elementary school principal. I can give her a call and maybe she'll talk with you on the QT. I'll wait till seven-ish to call her, and then let ya know. All about who ya know, not what ya know, right?"

"That'll be great, Roz. Thanks," Phoebe had to agree, even though Hank was a high school kid, not elementary. "Close enough for a start. Now, what's the scoop on the wife?"

"I thought you were fishin' for information last night at the Club. I'll tell ya, sister, the internet is an amazing, free 'n' fast vehicle, ya know? You should try it sometime," Roz kidded.

"Sure beats a million phone calls and begging the local library for their help," Phoebe nodded. "When I lived in Salt Lake, I had the church librarian on my speed dial. But I gotta pay attention to this road. Did ya find anything?"

"Oh, sister, I tell ya, turns out there's a wife for sure, no divorce legal-wise anyway. And there's a house in both their names. The whole nine yards, but no sign of kids, and no IRS claim of dependents. Ever. I'll tell ya, other than the house and an old, old marriage certificate, there's no outward sign of them bein' married—havin' kids, sharin' cars, or openin' bank accounts in both names. Nada. Must've been a secret or somethin'. I used to hear of first cousins marryin' in secret, but it was out of necessity down on the bayou waters where I grew up. Not a lot of candidates to choose from down there, ya know?"

"Wow, you're amazing and it's way early, Roz," Phoebe admired while also noting a herd of buffalo in the pasture along the highway. "Did you happen to get a full name for the wifey? Address? Bralette size? No, just kidding. But you've saved me hours. How do ya do this?"

"Okay. Okay. A lady never tells and I'm keepin' it that way," Roz laughed. "It's just that on last year's taxes she was still working at some radiator repair shop. She's been there a loooong time from the looks of the records. Interestin' to note, Old Al doesn't show up to the IRS. It's like he totally dropped out at some point. I'm limited to about the last fifteen years or so when it comes to my buddies at the IRS."

Roz confirmed the name—Martha Lewis—and gave Phoebe both work and home addresses for her. *I'll see you shortly, Old Al's wife of record,* Phoebe almost whispered.

DAMSEL IN DE-STRESS

As the SUV rolled on down the highway, Phoebe could feel her muscles start to relax. The hundred miles or so were all two-lane secondary highways, and would be slow going whether at the speed limit of 65 mph or edging a bit to 70. Two hours of driving would give her time to plan her talk with the wife. If she got in to see the elementary school principal, she would be ready for a talk with her as well.

When Phoebe rolled into Greenstone, she understood how it got its name. When the town was built, they must have used every ounce of the locally quarried stuff to build the town. It was everywhere—as the main ingredient for walls, bridges, the post office, churches, an old section of the elementary school, you name it. The local Chamber of Commerce had the presence of mind to encourage the preservation of the old buildings, and Main Street became a National Historic District. There were flowers still in bloom, even at the end of summer. It appeared all the hotels were full. "No Vacancy" signs sparkled over the mountainside, reflecting the morning sun. Banners hung across the business route, advertising the Labor Day weekend Art Festival. *Welcome to Historic Greenstone, population 5,042.*

A stop at the one and only elementary school to meet with Roz's friend, Laurie Watson, was set for mid-morning when the kids would all be safely tucked away in their classrooms. Her first stop, however, had to be the Greenstone Police Department to introduce herself. There was nothing worse than an out of town Sheriff's Unit roaming around the city uninvited.

The cop shop was centrally located in the small town and just a few blocks from the Carnegie Library and the Greenstone Elementary School. Phoebe thought about a pitstop at the Carnegie, as it was rare to see a functioning Carnegie anymore, and a library is usually an easy place to check out the bathroom facilities.

She could tell a lot about a community just from their library, and a Carnegie states the flavor of the community. Up on the steep hill, their Carnegie looked tired. Parking was nonexistent, and to add insult to injury, you had to actually park down the hill on the street, then walk up the hill to the main door for the book drop. *Humph,* she thought. *What gives with this? How do they get away with the lack of handicap access? Think I'll skip the stop and their bathroom.* Instead, she pulled into the parking lot in front of the cop shop and parked near the door. It would be just a short few-minute visit, or so she assumed.

Phoebe hustled through the front door and rang a buzzer on the wall for attention. *It could be no one is around, as early morning is prime coffee and donut time.*

After a few minutes, she heard someone ask, "Hello, what can we do for you?" There was a camera and a speaker in a corner of the ceiling that must have been how they could see her and reply to the buzzer.

"Hello," Phoebe hesitated, wondering how loud she needed to speak to be heard and where she should aim her voice. "I'm a visiting officer from Green County and just stopped in to introduce myself."

"Hold right there," the ceiling boomed again, "and someone will be out to meet you."

A few minutes passed, and a door off to her side was suddenly jerked open. She turned at the sound. There stood the most beautiful man she had seen in recent memory, maybe the most beautiful one ever. At that very moment, she choked on who knows what and went into a coughing fit, complete with gagging and spitting. Her eyes started to stream, and her nose suddenly gushed like someone had flushed her sinus cavities. The beautiful man stepped up to her and started pounding on her back while simultaneously pulling out a handkerchief to press against her face. That sent her into panic mode, and the coughing got worse. Suddenly, her snorting went silent as her throat burned and then closed. Eyes bugging out of her head, she could not catch an ounce of air.

The beautiful man calmly tapped his shoulder mic and called dispatch for a fire department medic to be sent over. The next few minutes were crazy and loud. In her shock at the chaos coupled with the throat event leading to shortness of oxygen, her legs, stiff and tight from the long car ride, gave out. Down she went, only to be caught by the beautiful man—the fall looking more like a swoon. Maybe even like a ladylike swoon, but as she passed out, she was thinking, *Probably not so much. Welcome to Historic Greenstone, Officer Phoebe.*

The fire department was co-located twenty feet from the police department. All of the first responders were delighted to practice their skills, albeit in the tiny closet-like space—packed in like the proverbial sardines.

In the case of help for Phoebe, it was the Perfect Storm. Her discombobulation was over nearly as fast as it started, and she refused the offer of a ride over to the Pikeview hospital. Phoebe knew her law enforcement guidelines, and by calling it a "situation" as opposed to an "event," no papers needed to be written up or forwarded to Sheriff Joe.

Her cough had subsided, and everybody agreed she would be fine, a tad blushed with embarrassment but fully recovered from the situation with the help of the beautiful man supporting her head with one hand, and holding her hand with his other.

"Beautiful Man" coaxed her to join him for a bit of food and a hot cup of coffee. It was the least he could do, as he assumed his sudden appearance had startled her, thus triggering the embarrassing incident. The medics surmised that a twenty-ounce black coffee on an empty stomach, coupled with the long car ride had ill-prepared her for a bit of a shock.

Suspecting there would be a quick call to her sheriff back in Oresville, she cleverly avoided questions like, "What brings you to our fair hamlet?"

Phoebe and her beautiful man walked next door to the Buckhorn Saloon & Good Karma Coffee Shop. She could not help but look around and wonder about such a combination of business enterprises. *Small town improvisation*, she guessed. It was a comfortable spot, or was it the company at the table? In an effort to cover her embarrassment and get warmed up from the inside out, she guzzled coffee in between bites of an egg sandwich.

Though her beautiful man had mentioned his name, Phoebe could not remember it for the life of her. She put on her best smile, opened her eyes wide, angled her head, and kiddingly said, "So Officer, let's start over, what d'ya say? I'm Phoebe Korneal and you are?"

With that thinly veiled attempt to get names straightened out, beautiful Officer Masterson smiled, revealing perfect teeth.

"Around the station, I'm called Batty," was his flushed-face reply.

She hoped the nickname did not come from some weird animal-related practice. Perhaps he was a terrific softball player—he certainly had the bulging shoulders beneath the cop shirt. Her detective mind back in the game, Phoebe was interested in how his nickname came about. To put him at ease, she told him her alias was "Fifi" and how it followed her from Salt Lake to Oresville.

Feeling comfortable, Batty went on to explain the Masterson family. He was guessing that his mother, in a very weak moment, named him after her American West Hero, Bat Masterson. The real Bat Masterson was a gambler, journalist, Army scout, buffalo hunter, and lawman who spent time in Denver and up and down the Colorado Front Range.

Born Bartholomew William Barclay Masterson, Batty was no relation to the old west hero and was about as far removed in his accomplishments and career path from the famous Bat Masterson as he could be, except for the lawman part, at least so far in his thirty years. His friends, he noted with an inviting smile, called him Bart.

While they were comparing notes on police work, personal histories, and choices around coffee types, the subject of the local Klingfus family came up. Phoebe explained she was in town to get some background on Hank Klingfus, a new kid to the Oresville area, who appeared to be living off the grid. She did not mention the school she was headed to was the elementary school, which would make no sense whatsoever since Hank was a *high school* dropout, not an elementary school dropout. She did not mention Old Al or Hank's relationship with him. That could wait.

Bart shared with Phoebe that the Klingfus family was just an ordinary family. No run-ins with law enforcement, but they stood out as having several kids, and the kids were self-described as being "free spirits." In short, Bart knew the oldest, Hank Williams, had left town, and the remaining three kids were pretty much being their free-spirited selves on the streets, enjoying summer in the city parks, and apparently not going to school. School had only been in session three weeks and Bart had already called on the parents regarding the kids' absence from classes. Phoebe was getting the picture and had personal experience with parents who didn't bother to enforce school attendance. Every town had the occasional "free spirit family."

An hour later, Phoebe and Batty-Bart agreed they had to get back to work. They parted just outside the doorway of the saloon and coffee shop. Bart asked if she ever came to Greenstone in her free time.

Phoebe answered, "I seldom ask for two days off in a row. The other officers are family men and need their weekends with their kids and wives." Looking him directly in the eye, she added, "So far, that is." They were nearly the same height and, *Geez, he really is a beautiful man! Shiny black hair pulled into a short ponytail, Irish blue eyes, smooth, fair skin . . . Ahhhh . . . Snap out of it!*

Phoebe had not been in a relationship since she had moved to Oresville and had no desire to start down that road. She had enjoyed some occasional companionship, but her job was a stumbling point. She loved what she did, and it always came first in her life. Some men did not view that as a tolerable arrangement. Phoebe and her friends were living life free and single.

Bart hesitated and offered slowly, "Okay. How about a phone number for you so I can update you with any news about the Klingfus family?"

"Sold," said Phoebe, and she handed him her Green County business card. Walking to her vehicle, she pondered. *What is this, Phoebe Korneal?*

Distracted as she was, she drove the short distance to the elementary school to meet up with Roz's friend, Principal Laurie Watson.

Laurie welcomed Phoebe into her office. The conversation started with Phoebe updating Laurie on Roz, and Laurie expressing her excitement about the smooth start of the new school year just three weeks back. The principal was dressed like everyone's favorite fun aunt. She wore a red gingham vest with Disney characters sewn on each side, over a soft fabric blouse, along with a long denim skirt. Her laced-up black shoes with sturdy soles gave her that Mary Poppins flair. Phoebe wondered how such an unstylish schoolmarm could be stylish Roz's friend.

Phoebe finally got around to the real reason for her visit—mining for information on the Klingfus family. She told Laurie that Hank Klingfus appeared to be living off the grid, and that he seemed young for his age and ought to be in high school. Laurie agreed and reconfirmed what Phoebe had heard earlier from Officer Masterson—the Klingfus kids were on their own and the parents could be described as old hippies or hippie wannabes, if "hippie" was still a term.

"There are four Klingfus kids, in all," Laurie began. "Hank, the oldest, dropped out of school this summer and took off. Since then, the other three have been on their own. Technically, they're not neglected, just encouraged to make their own good decisions. That's the Klingfus' philosophy."

Laurie knew Hank personally, as he had been in a tenth-grade history class she taught in the high school before she took the job as principal of the elementary school. Her assessment of Hank back then was that he was a quiet kid, and perhaps a bit socially immature. He had the usual few friends and was overwhelmingly honest.

Ditto on the immature part, Phoebe thought, and she added the honesty part to her mental file on Hank.

Shaking hands, Phoebe thanked Principal Laurie for her time and invited her to Oresville for skiing in the coming season. The Old Farmer's Almanac was promising a lot of snow, and skiing would be great.

Gracefully adjusting her duty belt and bulletproof vest, she then took her leave, heading to Pikeview and the work address Roz had given her for Martha Lewis. Adjoining towns, any boundary between Pikeview and Greenstone was non-existent. The image of Greenstone and one beautiful Officer Batty remained burned in her mind.

PICKING UP STEAM

Phoebe found herself in the industrial part of Pikeview, surrounded by lots of rectangular gray buildings—warehouses, mechanics' garages, commercial showrooms, and the lone radiator shop next to a vacant auto parts store.

That was easy enough, Phoebe thought as she parked and walked up to the entrance of Radiators-R-Us. Entering the front door, she looked for anyone who could help her. Past the empty front desk, back in the shop area, she saw a guy with his head eclipsed by the front end of a large truck. She called to him, asking, "Is Martha Lewis here?"

Looking up at Phoebe, the mechanic shook his head and grumbled, "She's been off the last four days, lady. I'm hoping she'll be back tomorrow. This backlog won't get done by itself! You'd think she'd know that, being the owner and all."

"Thanks," said Phoebe. *Owner, huh? Next stop, Martha's home address.*

Five minutes later, she was cruising down Maple Street in a nice, middle-class neighborhood. *Must be some money to be made in radiators,* thought Phoebe. Pulling up in front of a neat ranch home landscaped to perfection, she parked the SUV and strolled up the driveway. An older Camry sat to the right of the house. The door of the standalone garage that sat back on the lot, stood open, revealing two motorcycles parked side-by-side. *No wonder she doesn't park her car in the garage.*

Stepping up to the front door, Phoebe rang the bell. The door jerked open and there stood a tall, heavyset woman with a questioning look on her face. "What's up? What can I do for ya?"

"My name is Phoebe Korneal, and I'm a deputy with the Green County Sheriff's office. Are you Martha Lewis?"

"Yes, I am, but everyone calls me Queennie. What brings ya here?" the woman in tight jeans, dish towel in hand, extended a warm welcome.

"Are you related to Al Lewis?" Phoebe inquired.

"Yes, as a matter of fact, I'm his wife. Last time I checked, anyways," she grimaced with a bit of a huff as if she had made a small joke.

"Queennie, we need to talk," Phoebe encouraged. "May I please come in? I have some information for you."

"Sure," said Queennie, as she stepped back from the entryway. "Come in 'n' have a seat. Care for a cuppa? I was just taking a break from some work on one of my bikes and tending to some work in the kitchen."

"Thanks," Phoebe replied, "Coffee, black, would be great."

Queennie reached for the tiny cigar burning in the ashtray on the coffee table, and swinging her dish towel, gestured Phoebe to a comfy, old armchair, "Sit. Sit. Sit." She then disappeared into the kitchen to pour them both a cup of coffee.

Phoebe took the opportunity to look around. She could see the dining area, the short hallway to the kitchen, and another hallway to the left. Everything was spotless. And spartan. There was everything one needed, but not one extra thing. Queennie appeared to be a terrific housekeeper and a minimalist. *Interesting.*

Returning from the kitchen, Queennie placed a tray with two cups of coffee, creamer, and sugar bowl on the table.

Queennie? thought Phoebe. *How did she get to that from the name Martha? Could this be someone else? Doubtful. This is the worst part of this job. Maybe I should help myself to cream and sugar to delay the delivery of this bad news. Maybe she didn't hear I said coffee "black." I could start adding cream to my morning coffee to make up for a lack of breakfast. I wonder if it would cover as breakfast, or at least check the box and save on calories?*

Interrupting Phoebe's wandering thoughts, Queennie asked again, "So what's up? Why do you want to know if I'm related to Albert?"

Phoebe remembered her detective training from Salt Lake City—look for a "tell" and always use the same name the interviewee uses for the discussion. "I'm afraid I have some bad news for you, Queennie. Albert was found at the Sunshine mine yesterday morning. He's dead."

"Dead? Couldn't be. I just saw him yesterday and he was fine. Maybe not feeling great, but not feeling real bad." The stoutly woman took a deep drag from her More cigarillo.

Phoebe was still hanging on the comment about "yesterday." *How was that possible?* She cleared her throat and went on, "Queennie, I'm so sorry for your loss. There's no doubt here. Albert has passed away."

As Phoebe observed Queennie, she could see her denial turn into realization as she folded into herself on the couch in shock. "What happened to him? Did a bear get 'im?"

"No," Phoebe specified, "not a bear. Actually, his body is undergoing an autopsy right now to determine the cause of death. The preliminary report noted a bruise on his back, but nothing that would have killed him. We're hoping to get the final report by tomorrow morning."

Staring at Phoebe, Queennie was silent. Her mouth hung open with a silent cry as she struggled to absorb the information. Emotions flashed across her face—shock, followed by the furious blinking of tears being held back, and then gulping air, all of which quickly changed to a scrunched, pinched look of anger on Queennie's face, almost like she had just figured out what Phoebe had said.

"Well, he left me once and now he's gone and left me again! I guess there's no hope he'll be coming back this time." She sucked hard on the cigarillo, creased her eyebrows together, and then, with a sudden exhale, stared at Phoebe like she was expecting a correction.

"No, not this time, Queennie. Is there anything I can do for you?" Phoebe was experienced with notifying next of kin, but it was never easy.

"I don't think so. Actually, I can hardly think at all." With all her weight, Queennie-Martha sank further into the couch and took a shaky breath, "You know, I've loved him all my life, but our life together was just not meant to be. Did you know him well, Officer?"

"No, I can't say I did. We chatted once in a while at the Elks Club, but he wasn't an easy man to get to know. Loved his privacy and time up in the mountains with Rose." Phoebe waited for the seemingly devastated woman to respond. Though the quiet was comforting, Phoebe wanted her to talk. Queennie had said that she'd seen him yesterday, and Phoebe wanted the story on that visit. Could this woman be a person of interest? The spouse was always the first suspect.

Finally, Queennie puffed out her cheeks, slowly blew out a breath of smoke, and sadly said, "You got that right."

She looked off across the room and started to tell Phoebe the story of Albert and Martha . . .

They met when she was in her teens and they fell in love. Martha thought Albert was handsome and smart. Thanks to the GI Bill, he was studying to become a geological engineer. She felt fortunate to have found the man of her dreams, the one who would allow her to become the wife, mother, and homemaker she always wanted to be, while he pursued his engineering degree and then a career. Albert thought he could become a good husband to his strong, independent Martha. He did love her. But Albert still couldn't let go of the very different life he envisioned.

He dreamed of leaving engineering as soon as possible, living in the mountains, and mining for gold. No children, no happy little ranch house in the suburbs, no playing bridge with the neighborhood couples, no enjoying backyard barbeques with his family. Of course, they never discussed those dreams before they married the month after Albert graduated from college. They both looked forward to the future . . . just not the same future.

Albert quickly realized that married life with the accompanying domestication was not for him. He cherished his solitude and, although he loved Martha, could not handle living with her in the 'burbs. One day he told her he could no longer live in Pikeview, and that he was leaving for the mountains above Oresville. The Moly mine up there was hiring, and as a miner at heart and a loner, he just had to go. There was a promise to always take care of her, "Don't worry about money, Martha."

Martha was heartbroken. Her dreams of a family blew in the wind. Her whole life was turned upside-down. *How can this be? How can he leave me like this? What will I do?* she wondered. But, being the self-reliant person that she was, she picked herself up, dusted herself off, and clicked the "New Dream" button in her brain. *If I can't be a homemaker, mother, and devoted wife, what will I be?*

Martha had grown up with a dad who was a master mechanic. He felt it was important for all of his children, both boys and girls, to understand the mechanics and components of an automobile. As a result, one thing she knew about was cars, trucks, and motorcycles, and that included engines, radiators, and tires. If it had wheels, Martha was all about it. So, she looked in the Help Wanted section of the newspaper and the rest was history. She went from a worker in a small radiator shop to the owner/manager/occasional worker. Martha-Queennie was quite the woman!

"You mentioned you saw Albert a day ago. Where was that?" asked Phoebe.

"Albert always gives me money in the spring, but this summer I needed some extra. I want to expand my shop. Always more business than I can handle, and I have a chance to buy the vacant shop next to mine. So, I took the Beemer to the Sunshine to meet him where we always meet."

Phoebe stopped her right there, "Your Beemer is a car?"

"No," she corrected Phoebe, "it's a BMW motorcycle. An adventure bike, both off-road and highway. I bought it new back in 2011 when they first came out. Do you ride?"

"No. Just trying to understand how you got to the Sunshine. Please continue," Phoebe smiled encouragingly.

"Well, we had talked on the phone and agreed to the time on late Sunday afternoon," Queennie explained. "We usually touch base every few months. He calls my cell phone when he's near a phone up there in Oresville."

Phoebe noted that Queennie spoke of Old Al in present tense, an indicator she hadn't had time as yet to adjust to him being gone. *It's more likely that she just found out, making her less likely to have been involved in his death.*

"He was there when I arrived," Queennie continued, "and he looked fine. Maybe a bit older than usual, but nothing that made me worry. He's a few years older than I am, ya know. We sat in front of the mine and had a glass or two of wine. Of course, this led to us arguing about how much money I needed.

I'm afraid Albert and I can get to arguing pretty fast. I was angry. He was making me beg for the money, so I got up from my chair and told him I was leaving and never wanted to see him again, and he could keep his precious money. He came after me and, as I tried to get on my bike, reached over it and grabbed my arm. I leaned into the bike and it fell toward him, hard. It hit his back and down he went, with the bike on top of him.

I was so sorry. My bike is a heavy sucker. I hauled the bike off him, helping him sit up. I asked him if he was okay. He said he was and let's not fight anymore. So, we went back to the chairs. I poured us another glass of wine. He seemed to be just a bit uncomfortable but didn't complain. Then, he reached into his jeans pocket and took out the money I needed."

"How did he give you the money, Queennie? Cash or a check?" Phoebe flipped to a new page in her notebook.

"Neither. Albert doesn't believe in banks, and he doesn't carry much cash. He always gives me the money in gold coins."

Phoebe nearly fell out of her chair. *Gold coins! How did Queennie convert them to dollars? And, more importantly, how did one of them get under Old Al?* She decided to wait for the rest of the story.

Queenie continued, "We decided to watch the sun go down over the mountain, and one thing led to another.

We might not have been able to live together, but we always had a desire for each other. So, I spent the night in his sleeping bag at the mouth of the Sunshine. When I got up at dawn the next morning, I tidied up the area and left. I can tell you for sure that when I left, Albert was alive and well."

What a turn of events. Queennie, up at the Sunshine. Albert with gold coins. Phoebe's head was spinning. *I've got to take some time to put this all together,* she thought. Just then her phone rang.

"Hi, Phoebe," the caller cleared his throat, "it's me, Officer Bart, over in Greenstone. We met this morning? Well, anyways, I just found out the Klingfus kids are still not going to school. So, I'm going to make a house call on the parents. Wondering if you would like to join me?" He was nervous, and all of his words came out without taking a breath.

Phoebe had much to do trying to put this new information into perspective, but something wouldn't let her say no. "I'm just finishing up here in Pikeview. I can be over your way in thirty minutes. Meet you at the station?"

"Great. See you then," and he hung up.

Apologizing to Queennie for cutting her visit short, Phoebe asked if there was anything she could do to help before leaving. Queennie shook her head, but added that she would look forward to Phoebe's call when Albert's body was going to be released. Phoebe picked up the coffee tray to help anyway. Queennie followed her into the kitchen where Phoebe nearly dropped the tray when she saw what was on Queennie's kitchen counter. There sat several stacks of bright, shiny coins, lined up for the world to see.

"Queennie," Phoebe tried to sound casual, "what are those doing on your counter?"

"Just cleaning them before I cash them out," Queennie answered.

"May I look at them more closely?" Phoebe asked.

"Sure," Queennie nodded toward the counter.

Phoebe picked up a stack of five coins to examine. And there it was, the stamp of "The Last Hurrah" on one side of a coin and "2014" on the other. Exactly like the coin she had found under Old Al at the Sunshine.

"What do the numbers mean? Do they indicate the value of the coin?" Phoebe probed.

"No," Queennie explained, "it's not the value. It's the year the coin was made."

This situation gets more and more tangled, thought Phoebe. *I've got to get some thinking time in, and quick. The ride home will help.*

After once again sharing her condolences with Queennie, Phoebe headed out the door. Her phone rang again. *What now?* she mused as she hustled to the SUV. Answering, she found she was talking to Doc Watson.

"Phoebe, I have some info for you. Looks like Old Al died of arsenic poisoning from a long-time ingestion of it. Strange, but for sure it wasn't just a one-time shot."

"Arsenic, for sure? Where would he be exposed to arsenic unless someone was intentionally giving it to him?

We need to do some testing in the areas where he usually traveled, and perhaps we should check with Augusta." Phoebe added, "Doc, have you ever noticed how answers to questions seem to create more questions than answers?"

Doc agreed, "I'm thinking that since Old Al spent a lot of time at Augusta's mine, we might have to alert her to the possibility of arsenic in her area. What I'd like to do is some testing of any water at both mines—rivers, streams, wells. Just wanted to check with you first. I did talk with the sheriff and he said you've got the call on this."

"Thanks, Doc." *One more piece of this crazy puzzle that doesn't fit,* she thought. "Let's go ahead with the testing. Want me to make some calls from down here in Pikeview?"

"No thanks, Phoebe. I can get on this easier from up here."

The two talked a few more minutes about the bruise on Old Al's back. Doc reported that just as he had suspected from the preliminary autopsy report, the bruise was not related to Al's demise.

"Okay," Phoebe was ready to wrap up the call, "I'll fill you in with what I learn today. Let's compare notes tomorrow morning. In the meanwhile, I have one more visit to make in Greenstone while I'm down here."

They hung up and Phoebe continued her drive back to Greenstone with much to think about. With volumes of information filling her mind, she marveled that her concentration was so muddled by the intrusion of thoughts about whom she was going to meet—the Beautiful Man. *Stop it, Phoebe!* her better senses chided. *You have a murder to solve.*

Arriving at the Greenstone Police Station, Phoebe saw Bart standing by his SUV, waiting for her to arrive. As she pulled in to park, he gestured to her to join him.

Clearing his throat, Bart insisted, "Let's take my car to the Kingflus' home. More official in this town."

My God, he is beautiful, she thought, and practically vaulted from her front seat to his, kicking the hodgepodge of organic burrito and granola bar wrappers out of her way.

"No problem." Phoebe tried very hard not to stare at him. *I've got to focus on all these pieces and figure out how this poisoning happened to Old Al.*

"Phoebe, I'm glad you could come along on this visit. Maybe it won't seem quite so intimidating, you know, with someone as, well, you know, pretty as you are."

"Really, Bart? Intimidating or not, all I know is these kids and the one in Orcaville should be in school. Let's find out what's going on."

"Sure, Phoebe. Got it." But to himself he thought, *Oh great. Now I've offended her. Can't I ever say the right thing to a woman?*

They pulled up to the Klingfus house five minutes later, exited the car, and knocked on the door. Mrs. Klingfus answered, surprised to see two police officers on her front porch.

"Afternoon, Mrs. Klingfus. You remember me, Officer Masterson. And this is Officer Korneal from Oresville. We're here to talk about the kids not being in school again today. As we speak, both Loretta and Dolly are at the Memorial Park playground, and George is hangin' at the Arcade."

As the three of them talked, it became clear that the mom (likely the dad, as well), and the kids were on their own separate wavelengths. The mom hadn't known where the kids were. She assumed they were at school and was shocked to hear they were running around town. As for herself, she had lots going on at work and had just come home to pick up some papers. School days ended at just after three o'clock each day. The mom looked at her watch—*An hour to go. Nothing to worry about,* she thought.

She admitted the oldest son, Hank, usually ran the house and controlled his siblings. The family had not worked out a new routine since Hank had moved to Oresville.

"Hank is taking an Early Gap Year," Mrs. Klingfus informed them.

Bart and Phoebe exchanged glances. He raised his eyebrows for clarification, "An Early Gap Year?"

"I'll fill ya in later," mumbled Phoebe.

Mentally pointing and shaking her finger at the mom, she said in a strong, domineering voice, "These kids need to be in school by law, and currently they are not. You have until tomorrow to figure out whatever process you need to get them to school each day with or without Hank in the equation. It's. Your. Job."

The mom's mouth dropped open as she thought about how to respond. Ultimately, she agreed, "I'll make it happen." And stepping back, she went to close the door.

Phoebe added, "Mrs. Klingfus, don't make us come back here!"

As they walked to the cop car, Bart looked at Phoebe with a new respect, "You handled that exactly right! I've been here once already, and she didn't listen to me, nor did she do anything to fix the problem."

Phoebe raised both of her hands, "She's breaking the law and she knows it. She's the adult here, and moaning about Hank being gone doesn't get her off the hook. I guess I may have overreacted. Too much on my mind and I am starving. Can we get a late lunch or early dinner somewhere around here? I need to hit the road back to Oresville, but first, food."

Arriving back at the station house, Phoebe climbed into her own SUV and agreed to meet her beautiful man down the road at a Mexican joint, La Cocina.

While they sat eating tacos and enchiladas, Phoebe told Bart about the case she was working on in Oresville. As she voiced the story out loud, all the pieces started to fall into place.

She conveyed the details of the crime scene where they had found Old Al the day before. There was a coin under his body, and he was dressed like he was entertaining someone. And sure enough, he was. Al had a wife who lived in Pikeview, and she, Phoebe, had come to notify her of Old Al's passing and, of course, to check her out.

Bart offered, "Likely the wife did it. The statistics are nearly ninety percent of the time it is the spouse, or 'partner' as the term is coined. Right?"

"Right. However, there's more," Phoebe added to the mystery. "I thought that while I was headed to Pikeview to meet the wife, I'd stop by Greenstone to check out the kid, Hank, and his family history. He was Old Al's helper, or 'sherpa' as he was described. This, of course, led to my embarrassing meeting with you, Bart."

She smiled at Bart and continued to think out loud. "I could call the kid, Hank, suspect number one. He had worked for Old Al all summer. We thought he was the last person with Old Al until the wife admitted today that *she* was at the Sunshine meeting with Albert, asking for some extra money to help her expand her radiator business. They fought, made up, and she spent the night with him at the Sunshine. But she swore Albert was alive when she left him the next morning."

"So," Bart added, "now we are right back to 'the wife did it.'"

"Yes," said Phoebe, "except the person who found him and reported it was Augusta, who was a friend and maybe more to Old Al. Was she after the gold coin we found under Old Al's body? She says that she went to the

Sunshine to check on Old Al yesterday and give him a piece of her mind for the way he was treating the kid. Evidently, Hank had quit working for Old Al, went over to Augusta's mine, The Last Hurrah, and cried on her shoulder about what a sucker he felt like he was to have worked without pay all summer. He was full of self-pity, feeling like a failure, and he's broke."

Bart opined, "As is said, 'Follow the money.' Never a waste of time."

"Likely, and now back to the wife, Martha, who goes by 'Queennie.' She came to visit to get some money that she felt she deserved. Today I'm at Queennie's home and I spot gold coins. The coins were identical to the one we found under Old Al's body yesterday. The wife admits this is how Old Al gave her money because he didn't trust the banks. They do not deal in gold coins, which, by the way, are illegal if produced by individuals in this country. Could it be Queennie offed Old Al, grabbed whatever coins there were, and then rode her slick G650 Adventure Beemer back down to Pikeview?"

Bart whistled, "She's riding one of those? That's some big bucks."

"She also had an old Harley in the garage," Phoebe added. "I just happened to notice it when I was there today. Not bad. She loves her machines, I'd say."

"Wait!" Bart exclaimed, "The wife has a radiator shop, a Harley, and lives on the west side of Pikeview. Are we talking about Queennie Lewis?"

"Yes. She's exactly who we're talking about." Phoebe eyed him with interest. "Do you know her?"

"Not personally," Bart assured her, "but I'm familiar with her shop. Just connecting the dots here."

Getting back on track, Phoebe continued her story, "Now to top it off, the coroner calls and says there's no doubt about it, Old Al died from long term exposure to arsenic. So, was there someone trying to kill him off by purposefully giving him arsenic, or was his death an accident of nature? Not really death by natural causes, but wouldn't the EPA love to know about this?

The autopsy report noted the time of death was likely two to three hours before Doc arrived at the scene. This would fall into a timeline of Queennie leaving and Augusta arriving. It would also let suspect number one, the kid, off the hook." Phoebe stopped and took a deep breath.

Bart summed up what Phoebe had just recited, "Sounds to me like the only thing left is to figure out where Old Al was picking up the arsenic poisoning. The kid said Old Al was alive when he quit and left the campsite the day before yesterday. Queennie says he was alive when she left yesterday—evidently *very* much alive on the night the two of them spent together," Bart said with a blushing smile while looking directly into Phoebe's amber eyes. He went on, "Then, when his friend, Augusta, shows up, he's dead."

Phoebe met Bart's blue-eyed gaze, bit into another tortilla chip dripping with salsa, and smiled back. The paradigm seemed to shift as the pieces continued falling into place. "Thanks, Bart, I needed that. 'Follow the arsenic.'" And she laughed for the first time in two days.

FORK IN THE ROAD

Augusta woke up later than usual. Without looking out a window, it seemed too dark for six-thirty in the morning. Perhaps it was cloudy or foggy, or maybe fall had arrived overnight. The bad news and drama of Al's passing had taken its toll on her state of mind. She lay in bed for some extra minutes, mulling over the details and drama of the day before . . .

The evening had closed in fast as the sun sank behind the Massive. Bars of blue and pink streaked the sky and gradually blended into salmon colors as the air had cooled. A hoodie and coat were needed. Since the kid didn't have any warm clothes, Augusta had directed him to a plastic box of lost 'n' found items at the entrance to the mine.

"Help yourself to anything that fits. The box gets fuller every year and should probably be emptied," she guided him, thinking it was one less thing to pack up at summer's end. It wouldn't be long before she'd head into town for the winter, even though it was only the end of August. A scary thought. The Farmer's Almanac seemed to rule her choices for where to live at the altitude of 10-5.

The kid had layered enough to be warm, including a pair of Carhartt coveralls, baggy but long enough. Augusta had built a fire and they grilled hotdogs for supper. She was low on food, but hotdogs grilled over the fire always worked for a meal. He ate his fair share of eight dogs and a can of beans on the side. *Boy, could he eat!*

They were still sitting at the table as Augusta was finishing off a leftover sandwich from lunch and sipping her homemade Special Tea. She was calculating that if the kid stuck around, she would need to stock up on groceries in a big way. He ate fast, too, as if he were competing for a limited amount of food. Just the thought made her laugh out loud. It was truly an amazing sight, like a hotdog-eating contest. She couldn't help but think of the old TV scene of Lucy and Ethel slamming chocolates into their mouths in a candy factory assembly line.

Augusta's Special Tea was a simple homemade batch of gin made with her fresh well water. The recipe had been in her family for years. It was easy to make, fast to brew, and saved her weekly trips to the town's liquor store. She rationalized drinking way too much as an easy way to get her daily quota of water. Everyone knows to stay hydrated at that altitude. Al seemed to understand and helped himself when he stopped by, usually taking a jar with him when he left.

Dinner over, they had remained at the table, the kid trying to absorb the quiet after the drama of the day and Augusta hardly believing Al was gone. The last light of day saw no wind for a change, and the fire seemed to draw in the air as they took comfort in each other's company.

Listening carefully, she had let Hank talk. As an only child, she never knew what it was like to have siblings. His complaining about a brother and sisters was new to her. Her summer hires that year were from the Colorado School of Mines and the University of Kentucky. They were older kids, near graduation, and seldom talked about their families. But Hank was, well, a kid. Plus, he was young for his age. She had to admire his guts to leave home and his determination to learn the mining gig stuff from Al. His artless decision to quit school made her wonder what kind of parents would let him strike out on his own at such an early age. Where did he get the idea for an early gap year? Not an explanation that would go over really well on a resume. Most kids knew better than to leave home early, trading free room and board and a weekly allowance for the hardships of the work-or-don't-eat world.

As she had listened to him, she'd started to think about his age and whether there was a law requiring him to be in school. She would check out the state requirements on that. He said his classes in Greenstone started in early August—of course, without him.

Lying there in the dim light of the morning, thinking about her talk with Hank, one thought led to another for Augusta. She wondered if there were a way that she could convince him to return to school, family, and his friends. He'd have bragging rights of his great summer of camping and prospecting, the old guy he was learning from, and roaming the mountains at 10-5.

A summer of discovering mountain living around Oresville and the Arkansas Valley had done wonders for him. He was closer to six feet tall than when she had first met him with Al in late spring. His hair had grown long and was bleached by the sun. *Kind of shaggy, but it's the style, right?* He had a deep tan and probably the start of a hard case of melanoma by forty or fifty years old. *Teenagers don't carry sunblock-fifty anywhere.*

She could throw in a promise of summer work if he would return with his high school diploma, and not a GED. She decided to give it a stab, but the kid seemed a little slow on the uptake based on their talk that night. He seemed worried about finding his car to sleep in. On top of that, the mine wouldn't hire him without his diploma. He was flat broke without any pay from his summer with Al. To

Augusta, that had been the proverbial window of opportunity.

Catapulting out of bed with a plan, Augusta dressed for another day in the mountains. She would step into this situation head on. Looking out one of the Airstream windows, she could see the kid was moving around, probably hunting for something to eat.

A thin layer of frost covered everything as far as the eye could see. It was a chilly, quiet, mountain morning sans sun. She carried the coffee pot to the camp table and lit the Coleman gas stove for the start of ham and eggs. Rose, Al's mule, seemed to be fending for herself—one less thing to be concerned about. She didn't know much about mules, horses, teenagers, or men either, for that matter, as evidenced by several husbands in her wake.

The kid was already dressed and sitting at the table, looking at the black and white mountains.

"Ahem," she cleared her throat, "Morning, kid."

No response.

She handed him a mug of hot, black coffee, the steam swirling around his hand as he grasped the handle. Somewhat ungratefully, he handed it back to her. "I don't drink coffee without cream and sugar."

"Yeah, right." Augusta squinted her eyes, raised her eyebrows high, and looked directly at him with a cool stare. "How about we try this again? Morning, kid. Here's your first cup of decent coffee for the morning. And you say 'Thank you, Augusta.'"

Hank got the message and mumbled a "morning, thank you." He cupped the mug of coffee in both hands and made the best of it.

Hank was preoccupied with wondering how he could live in Oresville without a job, money, or a real place to sleep. His sleeping space in the hatchback of his car, Old Paint, was small at the start of summer, but he had grown. Squeezing his much taller body into the Pinto would be tough, and winter seemed to be coming down fast. Needing shorts, he had already cut off his high dollar Abercrombie jeans. If he went back to Greenstone, his Dad would likely hit the roof over ruining them, even though he had already outgrown them. And, if the kids back in Greenstone saw him in "high water" jeans, it would mean the immediate end to his high school social status.

"Okay," Augusta started again, "You know, kid, I hire college kids every spring for work in my mining operation up here. They've left now for their colleges, but some will be back next year for the summer. Would this be something you'd be interested in as a summer job next year?"

"I'm not a college kid," Hank pointed out, followed by a deep sigh. Staring into his coffee, he avoided looking at her.

"You'd have to have a high school diploma, but that's no biggie, right? The point is that you could move your Early Gap Year to after your senior year and spend it learning this mining business," she urged.

Augusta was starting to think long-term. The kid and his future college education could be a project for her, and she certainly had the money to help him. It sounded like his mom and dad had enough on their plates without adding college tuition to their budget.

"I guess I could go back to Greenstone," Hank grumbled and scuffed a rock from under the table. "School's not much, but it seems like no one will hire me without a diploma."

"Exactly." Augusta was beginning to think she was getting through to the kid. "You could get the diploma out of the way. Check that box, so to speak. And then come back up here next summer. Work for me, get paid, spend the summer in the mountains. Sounds like a plan, eh?"

"I think I could do that. It helps to know there's a job at the end of the high school stuff. But before I could go back to Greenstone, I thought you and I had agreed I'd take Rose and head over to your cabin today to check out how it's doin'." Hank was still thinking about the money owed to him and the possibility of it being at that cabin. "Without money from working for Al all summer, like, I can't go real far on an empty tank of gas, ya know?"

Hank may have been young for his age, but he was no dummy, or so he thought. Still, his thinking seemed to bounce around. If Al had been prospecting for years, there had to be gold somewhere. Of course, were he to find it there at the cabin, he would take only what he was owed for the summer of work.

Several times, Al had told Hank to sit tight and announced he was leaving to take care of business. Off on "The Hawk"—his 1968 Bushwhacker dirt bike—he would then show up later the same afternoon or the next day with more groceries. Because of that, Hank had assumed Al was just making a grocery run. Given what he was learning, however, perhaps Al was doing some other things, too. Like stashing the summer's gold?

Thoughtfully, Hank continued, "On Sunday, when Al had gotten back to our camp below the Sunshine, he didn't look so good. Kind of green around the gills, as my dad used to say. Plus, he wasn't gone all day, just a few hours first thing in the morning. I thought it wasn't the usual trip to town, but I was too busy thinking about quitting this gig to worry about Al's health or state of mind."

Augusta ignored the health observation. "I have no idea what he was up to. I think you're right. He owed you something for your help this summer. He never had a whole lotta cash as I could see, and I doubt he had a credit card or checkbook."

"I saw the gold dust and flakes we collected from the prospectin' we was doin'. He put every flake and every bit of dust into his beat-up old leather pouch. I wonder what happened to it."

With that said, Hank looked at Augusta to see if she would speculate on where Al may have kept it. Like they were reading each other's minds, they both turned their heads to look at Rose and the light saddle pack that was always on her back. They looked again at one another and stood from the table. Walking over to Rose, they flipped opened the saddle pack and reached in. The leather pouch was there . . . empty.

Augusta shrugged, "I know he didn't trust banks to hold it for him. They operate in money, not gold. No, where he kept it is probably one of those great mysteries of life." She tried to look as confused and clueless as Hank.

Augusta had a real good idea about *how* Al kept his gold, but *where* he kept his share of their little venture was not her business. Her partnership with Al over the years meant they both had a way of stashing their gold without the government getting their hands on it. She remembered her grandmom, Connie, and her mom, Anne Louise, telling her not to trust the government and to keep her money *liquid.* The Last Hurrah was mostly a silver mine with occasional gold mixed with the silver ore, and the Higgins ladies had their own way of processing what gold they accidentally mined each year.

The real Higgins' family money was tucked away and growing at a rapid clip back in Omaha. Augusta got an update every year in January during the Denver Stock Show. The money from her mining operations, however, was safely tucked away within her reach. She had practiced her mom's advice to "Keep your husbands close but your gold closer." Augusta and Al had figured out how to make that a reality.

Al had been one of Augusta's few friends. For years they had a loose partnership based on a handshake confirming their mutual understanding. With Al's engineering education and Augusta's family history, together they continued the Higgins' technique of protecting their gold—*coin it*. The tried and true way of keeping it safe without the aid of a bank or the watchful eyes of the federal and state governments. Their motto was "What they don't know won't hurt 'em."

The government had imposed a law prohibiting private ownership of gold—the Gold Prohibition Era of 1933 to 1974. When the law was passed, all citizens had to turn in their gold to the government. Augusta grew up listening to her mom, Anne Louise, complaining about the law at every opportunity or after one too many at the Club in Oresville. Any gold that her mother had was stashed away over the years with the help of Quinton Garrett, a retired assayer, hobby prospector, trusted life partner to Anne, and "Uncle Q" to Augusta.

Since great-granddad Sam Higgins, Augusta and the rest of the previous Higgins family ladies had practiced what he had perfected. When Sam started his mining adventure in the mid-1800s, depending on others to protect his gold was out of the question. A man could only trust his best friend, assayer, and blacksmith just so far. Being self-reliant was a necessity of life, and Sam used that philosophy to perfect turning his gold flakes, dust, and the occasional nuggets into hard coinage. The gold rush of Colorado was short lived, but Sam Higgins always found gold in his copper and silver mining operations. Old Al made sure that Sam's operation of coining gold lived on.

The beauty of gold coins was that they never corroded, tarnished, or reacted over time. Pure gold, being a soft metal, needed a bit of silver added to the mix to help stabilize it. If anyone tried to bite the coin as a test of counterfeit, it would be hard as a rock and pass the *taste test*. The other test was a marble shelf on the cash registers. The sound of a coin tapped on the marble plate above the cash drawer said a lot about the coin. It could tell the checker if it was an authentic gold coin or just a gold colored lead coin. Clink or clunk.

Augusta liked to think that stashing her gold as coinage was easier than hiding unlabeled jars in her kitchen cupboard for safe-keeping. She was a fast learner.

Al agreed with Augusta and took charge of the coinage process each winter. Great-granddad Sam's coining equipment was at the family homestead cabin. Al used Sam's refining crucible to melt the gold, and the rolling machine for the workable thickness of close to but not more than a fourth of an inch. The punching machine produced the shape, and then the die stamped "The Last Hurrah" onto the head side of each coin. Al's special touch was adding the year the gold was found to the tail side. He and Augusta had agreed an imperfect round coin was acceptable, so the edges were never milled.

By the time the sun's rays had enough strength to melt off the frosty covering, Hank and Rose were ready to head over to the Higgins' family homestead cabin. Augusta thought the trek would be a good test for the kid and give him the space to make some kind of a decision about whether or not he would take her up on her offer of an ongoing summer job. Assuming that would be possible, she tried to encourage him to think about something more than when his next meal was coming.

"Now remember," Augusta reminded him, "Rose knows where she is going, so if you get turned around, let her have her head and go along with it. She's been to the cabin with Al many times and knows the way. Mules are stubborn animals, so don't argue. Just let her go with her instincts, and you follow."

"Yeah, yeah. You've said this about a hundred times. Like this is some kind of big mystery." Hank's impatience was brewing.

This is a teenager, Augusta thought, as she took a deep breath and reminded herself to keep her own patience intact. "And what are we looking for over there?" she asked him.

"I'm supposed to see if the building is in good shape and report back to you. I don't know anything about taking care of a mule," he whined. "She pretty much was on her own this summer. Just carried stuff for us and ate whatever was around, ya know?"

"Okay, just make sure she has enough water, and be back here the day after tomorrow at the latest or I will come looking for you and bring a posse of hunters."

Augusta knew such an aimless kid needed a deadline for getting back to the Last, and a posse showing up would embarrass him. A few days without someone watching over him would be a good lesson. Maybe he would kick that Early Gap Year bullshit to the curb and head back to Greenstone as early as the weekend. She crossed her fingers, secretly hoping Hank didn't get too awfully lost.

Tapping him on the shoulder, Augusta pointed in the direction of the cabin. "Hit the trail, kid, and I'll see you in a couple of days."

As Hank walked down the forest service trail with Rose following, Augusta double-checked her brilliant idea. *I hope this is not one of my bigger mistakes*, she thought. Hank had one of her cell phones with him so he could call for help if he needed it. Her worry was eased by her favorite Al quote: "It is what it is."

Augusta headed back to the Airstream. Hank headed on down the trail toward the cabin, thinking about his new adventure. Tagging along behind him, Rose was giving the kid *the look*.

As Hank departed, Augusta gave herself the space she needed to process the Al situation. The quiet was comfortable—not her style. She decided to head to town for supplies and company at the Club. Maybe Carrie Jean had some news on Al's passing, and she could all around catch up.

Then there was the US Post Office mail delivery system in Oresville—a real problem for Augusta. The newest postmaster of the last couple of years seemed about half-baked. What could be so complicated about stopping the delivery to her mailbox at her house? Her discussions had gone nowhere with old Half-baked. The box always had mail in it during the summer, even though the Hold was always scheduled from May until October for more years than she could remember.

The last time she went to town, the box at her house was stuffed with packages and mail addressed to a family a block away. Old Half-baked had given her a hard look and walked away while she was mid-sentence complaining. "Half-baked" was probably an understatement. As Mom Anne Louise always said, "That dog don't hunt."

With her mom in mind, Augusta realized she had not gotten a letter from either her or Uncle Q all summer. That was not like her mom at all. She'd better head to town to fix the mail thing and, while there, handle some other things pending on her mind—a decent shot of her Pappy Van Winkle Whiskey, for one. Someone had given her a very expensive twelve-year-old Special Reserve bottle at the Stock Show in January. The Club was the safest place to keep it. She could use a taste of Pappy right then. Neat, of course.

THE DOCTOR IS IN

Doc Watson had received the results of the toxicology testing from the medical examiner. The final analysis had confirmed Al had died of long-term arsenic poisoning. Doc had suspected that would be the case when they had sent off the samples of the blood, tissues, and urine from the autopsy the day before. In his twenty years, he had only seen one other death caused by arsenic poisoning, but he remembered it well.

Dark brown patches discolored Old Al's stomach, chest, and back. The body had rough, patchy bumps or moles of some kind on the arms, wrists, and palms of his hands. Likely skin cancer. Having the tox report, he was able to link the skin discoloration and the bumps to signs of prolonged arsenic consumption. Even the fingernails had telltale streaks of whitish lines, again indicating arsenic. The internal organs, specifically the kidneys, were failing, and he was likely at an early Stage-4 level of hypertension.

They had ruled out the bruise on the back as a cause of death. At sixty-nine, Al was not getting any younger and prospecting was a tough way of life—apparently so was his sex life when it included motorcycle mamas with a slippery grip.

Doc called the district's health department to report arsenic as a cause of Al's death, and asked for a test of the city drinking water. As he waited for the call back, he sat and thought about Al and the life he had led. Certainly, the stream and lake water he consumed day after day was not in any way tested or treated. If not treated, Doc had to wonder if Al had ever been diagnosed with Giardiasis. Would he have gotten prolonged exposure to arsenic from any of those mountain waters?

Al was friends, and maybe more, with Augusta. Doc knew all about Augusta's Special Tea, but doubted the tea was intentionally laced with arsenic. However, any homemade brew can carry the arsenic if the water used is contaminated. If that were the case, she would have the same symptoms as Old Al.

It was time to add Phoebe to the conversation. However, as an elected official, he best be sure he had crossed every T and dotted every I. She needed to hear the results of the tox report, and then together they could decide on the next steps. Doc decided he would put in a call to Augusta to get a blood sample from her. If his theory was correct, she would need to be tested.

It was still early afternoon when Doc called the Sheriff's Department, only to be told that Phoebe was in Pikeview and could be reached on her cell. Roz sounded distracted, and Doc could hear her talking to someone else at her desk. Sheriff Joe picked up the line and asked Doc for any news. Doc explained he had both the autopsy and the tox results confirming that Al's death was due to long-term arsenic consumption.

"Well, then, this sounds final," Sheriff Joe concluded. "I'll leave it with you and Phoebe to work out the details." He hung up the phone. Doc got the message, loud and clear.

Phoebe answered Doc's call with anticipation. He could hear her breathing like she was walking fast somewhere outside. He explained the final analysis of the autopsy.

Phoebe fastened her seatbelt with a hard click. "Ahhh, okay, then. Anything about the bruise on his back? I know the prelim' report said it didn't cause the death, right?"

"Yup, it holds up. No fault with the bruise." Doc explained he had put in a call to the town's water department for an arsenic level test. Phoebe agreed. Erring on the side of caution was her style. They brainstormed about where the arsenic could have come from, given Old Al did not live in town. She also added that Old Al spent his winters at the Higgins' cabin, where there surely was a well. They agreed to track the arsenic via Augusta, The Last Hurrah mine, and her cabin. Those seemed to be the logical next steps.

Phoebe explained that she was leaving Queennie's house in Pikeview, had another stop to make, and planned to get back to Oresville late that night. They would touch base tomorrow.

Doc dialed Augusta's cell phone. "Hey, Augusta, this is Doc Watson over at the mortuary. Do you have a minute?"

"For you, always," Augusta replied sweetly.

"I'd like to ask you to stop by the town clinic in the next few days to let us run some tests to make sure you haven't been exposed to arsenic as Al was," Doc urged in a caring way.

As luck would have it, Augusta was already on her way to the post office in Oresville and agreed to make the clinic her first stop. He quickly called the clinic and told them what he wanted, arranging for the nurse practitioner to get a blood and urine sample to look for signs of arsenic, at no charge to Augusta. Instead, the testing and visit would get billed to the county. He requested they perform a physical exam to check for obvious signs of arsenic poisoning. He included another request for a breath test, as garlic breath is sometimes another indicator.

Sitting back in his ancient, cracked, crooked leather desk chair, Doc dissected the autopsy information and the tox report while he waited for the report to come in from the water department in Oresville. He was the county coroner, not the lead county official; however, he did share some leadership for the county and understood there was a certain amount of accountability with his job. Concluding he was on the right path, he made up his mind he would stay on the case until he was satisfied that he understood the source of Al's arsenic poisoning.

The call came back from the water department as "negatory." Nothing other than the usual trace of arsenic—definitely below the Environmental Protection Agency guidelines of 0.010 parts per million. He had been around long enough to remember the old EPA guideline as a bit higher, so the county had already met the newer requirements even before the revised drop-dead guideline in early 2006.

The town's carefully treated water was a combination of groundwater, well water, and snowmelt that came from east of Oresville, where the Mosquito Range ran into Evans Reservoir.

No, he thought, *Al's arsenic consumption came from elsewhere. Not the town's drinking water.*

Al had traveled and lived in the mountains, seldom showing up in town. He had the kid traveling with him that summer, so the working folks of Oresville saw less and less of him. When he did show up in town, it was without Rose or the kid.

Doc flashed on the kid. He knew the kid had been with Al all summer, and before that, wasn't living in Oresville. He figured he could test the kid, as well, to see what his levels were and compare the results to Al's levels on the tox report.

The ringing of Doc's phone brought him to attention. He put his suppositions on hold and answered, "Doc here. What can I do for you?"

"Hey, Doc, this is Lily, the PA over at the clinic. I've got Augusta here, and the analysis shows she has higher than safe levels of arsenic in her system. The other tests show she is healthy and nothing to worry about, so far. Do you want me to fax this report over to you?"

"Hummm," Doc pondered, "you can send the written report over and I guess Augusta is good to go. I need to do some work on this. You did a full tox screen on her? Blood, urine, and all?"

"Yup," Lily confirmed. "Some of the results will take a few days. But so far, everything is within limits, except for the arsenic. If she were to stop consuming it, in a few days another test would likely show a lower amount in her system. I know you're busy, but she wants to talk with you about what's goin' on. Should I have her stop by your office?"

"If she can wait a few minutes, I'll come to the clinic and talk with her there. That is, if she doesn't have anywhere she needs to be. We should talk about this arsenic situation. Is there a young kid with her? Like a teenager?" Doc was hoping for a double shot of good luck.

"No," replied Lily, "she's by herself. Can you come over right away? I'll ask her to stick around for a few, even though she's not real happy to be here."

"Please do. My office is only five minutes from the clinic and I'm headed out the door as we speak." He grabbed his sport coat off the back of his chair and practically ran out his office door.

Three minutes later, Doc walked into the clinic and over to Augusta who had a worried look on her face.

"What's up, Doc?" Augusta asked with a concerned look. "First Al dies, and now you've got me in here for tests. I haven't been sick in years, and I've never been to this new location for the clinic. It's been what, ten or twelve years since it opened?"

Doc motioned for Augusta to join him in a consultation room, and Lily followed close behind them.

"Augusta," Doc began with his best bedside manner, "you and I have known one another for a long time."

"And your point being?" she asked.

"We got the toxicology report back this morning from the autopsy on Al. It seems he died from arsenic poisoning. His internal organs just gave out. When I saw the report, I asked you to stop by the clinic so we could test you, too." Doc glanced at Lily, then returned his attention to Augusta.

"Augusta, you have an unusually high level of arsenic in your blood and urine," he continued. "Not all of the lab results are back yet. Some will take a few days. Can I ask you how you're feeling?"

Augusta looked at the PA and reported that she felt fine—never better, in fact.

Doc cleared his throat, "Augusta, when you spend the summers at the Last, where do you get your water?"

Augusta wrinkled her brow. "We have a well for our water and it has never gone dry all these years. Then I come into town for the winters. The Old Farmer's Almanac is forecasting an early winter this year, so I'll likely wrap things up at the mine and move back to town shortly."

"Do you know where Al got *his* water?" Doc rested a hand on Augusta's as a reassuring gesture.

"I assume from the streams and creek beds," she told him, noticing the warmth of his big, strong hand on hers. "I don't think he carried any water with him. Why bother when he was always working near water? I always refilled his half gallon jar with my Special Tea that I make at the Last. Just enough to enjoy at the end of each day when he was on the trail. He picked up a kid this summer to teach him the secrets of prospecting, but he's just a kid and too young to enjoy my tea," she laughed.

"Do you know where the kid is now, Augusta?"

"He headed over to my cabin this morning with Al's mule. I sent the mule with him to be sure he would get there and back without getting too lost." Again, she chuckled.

"Is there any way we could reach him?" Doc continued. "I'd like to test him for arsenic, too, since he's been with Al all summer. We'll need to test him as soon as we can get him here."

"Sure, I sent my extra cell phone with him. He should be at the cabin by now. I have a miniature hot spot up there on a trickle solar panel changer, so the cabin does have cell service. Let's give it a try." With that, she dialed Hank.

"Hey, kid, this is Augusta. We need you to come into town right away. Seems they have figured out what went on with Al." She listened and then added, "No, nothing like that. It appears he died of arsenic poisoning, and they want to see what a test of your blood might look like." She paused for a minute and then continued, "No, they're not thinking you poisoned him. Nothing like that," she laughed loud at his outlandish thinking.

Raising her eyebrows, Augusta gave a direct, questioning look to Doc, watching for his response to her words. Doc shook his head indicating a "no" and slightly smiled. Augusta seemed relieved.

She gave Hank some directions to the clinic, ended the call, and put her cell back into her coat pocket. While they were sitting there, she described the kid to Doc. She clarified that she called him "kid" though his real name was Hank, and although she had no idea what his last name was, she did know he needed to be back in high school in Greenstone.

Telling Doc that she had some errands to get done, Augusta let him know she'd be on her cell if he needed her. Gazing into his eyes for just a second too long, she smiled and excused herself.

On a mission, Augusta headed to the post office to see if she could fix that constant delivery loose end. Again!

EUREKA!

Hank and Rose made it to the Higgins' cabin with very few disagreements. Hank had learned Rose was a strong force to argue with, so he let the mule take the lead. When Al was around, the two of them seemed to have a silent language, and seldom did Hank hear Al get upset with Rose, or Rose get upset with Al, for that matter.

The trek over to the cabin was more of a hike, but after a summer of walking the mountains with Al, Hank was in great shape, so for him the walk was not much of a challenge. Augusta had told him it would take a half day to get there from the Last, but Hank made it in under two hours.

It was the first time the teenager had gone anywhere that summer by himself. Al had always been with him, giving instructions, positioning him at the wash plant to pour in the loose rock, showing him how to make meals, and shoring up the campfire. When he thought back over the last few months, he acknowledged it had all been a great learning experience. With that, the sound of his own voice echoed in his ears. Only Rose pretended to listen. Too quiet.

As he walked the trail, Hank kept thinking about the talk with Augusta. He didn't have a lot of options. Al was gone, so he could probably use Al's tools and camp gear to keep prospecting for another month or so. Augusta wouldn't hire him that late in the season. She would shortly close the Last for the winter and move to town. He could go, too, and try to find some local work. Sleeping in Old Paint was no problem until he had a stash of money for a room.

The *real* problem was that Oresville pretty much closed down in the winter. There was a ski area he could try, but the pay might not get him out of his car. They had already gotten some snow over the weekend, but a dusting in August wouldn't open a ski area in September, and he needed cash flow ASAP. His options were feeling more like a lack of options. Maybe he should go back to Greenstone, move back in with his family, and idle away the winter in school. Three hots and a cot, a few classes, and running the show with his sibs was sounding more and more appealing. As a big plus, he would have quite the stories to tell from his summer adventure, which would likely make him the senior class star.

When Hank walked up to the cabin, he noted the stillness of the secluded setting. Even the leaves on the aspens were silent. An invisible, reluctant breeze kicked up some dust, but no sound, no crackle of weeds as he stepped. Not even a snort from Rose as she led the way. Before too long, he noticed all the No Trespassing signs. Funny they were there, nailed to the occasional tree, like an advertisement for a cabin in that stand of aspens.

Closer to the log cabin, Hank could see the different additions Augusta's great-grandfather had built over the years. The whole thing appeared to be several sections of log rooms cobbled together. There were painted plywood boards on tracks across the top of each window. He supposed those protected the windows from the weather and vandals. Some of the boards appeared to be newer and with brighter colors than others.

He thought it strange there were no weeds around the cabin, even though it had stood empty all summer. He spotted some cans of paint, insecticides, and weed killer under a lean-to shelter on the south side of the cabin. Rose headed over to the shelter like it was *her spot*. In the yard, there was a deep well hand pump on a cracked concrete slab about ten feet from the front door. A tin cup hung on a chain from the side.

The cabin door consisted of sturdy rough-cut tree slabs fastened together with crisscrossing steel straps. A steel bar crossed the door, bearing a padlock that looked not only ancient but also bearproof. Above the door, a log with faded, shallow, roughly carved lettering read "Higgins 1860."

Hank was hungry, and there wasn't anyone around to fix him something to eat. He only had a few food items for the short visit to the cabin, but what the hell. He was on his own and could do whatever he wanted, so he decided to just stop right there at the doorstep and have a little snack. Ten minutes later he had devoured most of the loaf of bread and all of the peanut butter. He added some bananas to the first and second sandwich and washed it all down with the sun tea Augusta had sent with him.

Finishing his meal and stashing the leftovers in his pack, he turned Augusta's key in the padlock, pushed open the door, and looked around the first room before he stepped inside. It looked like a spooky place—dark, empty, dusty, and isolated. It felt even quieter inside the cabin than outside, if that was possible. Cautiously, he stepped into the Higgins' family kitchen.

As his eyes adjusted to the dim light, Hank reminded himself what he had come to the cabin to do for Augusta, as well as for himself. It was cool in the cabin. The walls looked tight, leaving no spaces for sunshine to sneak into the room, so he used an old brick to keep the door wide open and surveyed the rest of the rooms.

Every room was empty, except for a neatly made bed with a heavy quilt in one of the rooms. The kitchen was large, accommodating a giant wood-burning stove, a sink with a cast iron hand pump at one end, cupboards on two of the walls, a giant, solid wood, well-used chopping block in the middle of the room near the stove, and a large round table surrounded by six hand-carved high-back chairs made of pine. He noticed that one chair appeared to have butt marks on the dusty seat, and the table space was smooth and clean like someone had recently sat there and brushed the dust off just that spot. Hank thought about how Al had left their camp for a few hours the day before he died—maybe his butt had been there.

Prospecting the hills all summer together, he and Al had found plenty of gold. It had to be somewhere. Hank plopped himself into the chair and looked around the kitchen. *Where would I put the gold?* Standing up again, he started to search first the kitchen, then the other rooms. Tapping the floors with his foot, he listened for a hollow sound. The entire floor sounded hollow, though there was no sign of a door to a cellar or crawlspace.

After an hour of looking in every nook and cranny of the old cabin, he sat down again at a total loss for ideas. The phone Augusta had given him when he left the Last, startled him when it rang. It was Augusta telling him that she wanted him to come to town right away.

He looked down again at the wooden floor. The sun had hit high noon, sending bright shafts of light through the doorway into the kitchen. They swept the floor just right to highlight a crooked board appearing to be cleaner than the others. Saying nothing about what he was really up to, he assured Augusta that he and Rose would head to town, about a four-hour trek, and hung up the phone.

In no rush to start another hike, Hank knelt down to check the odd-looking board and went to work trying to pry it up from the floor. Sure enough, in a cubby below the floorboard, there were gold flakes and dust in a small pickle jar. Next to the jar were several boxes with coins in each of them. Lots of coins. He was right. It was a relief to know his work with Al was not wasted. Sure, he had learned some good mining stuff, but he needed money and felt that part of what he was looking at deserved to be his.

Pulling out one of the boxes, Hank examined each coin. He could see the markings on them—"The Last Hurrah"—with sunshine streaks bolting out from behind the words. There was a number stamped on the flip side. The first one read "2013" and the next one read "2014."

This could be Al's gold! Should I take a coin or maybe two? He contemplated his dilemma. *Maybe one for each week of the summer I worked for Al? Should I take the little jar of gold dust and flakes? If I do that, what would I do with loose gold? Like Augusta said, banks deal in money, not gold, and I need real money. Should I talk with Augusta first? This all might be her gold. It's her cabin, after all.*

Hank sat on the floor, and in the sunshine from the opened door, he turned those questions over and around in his brain. Then his conscience kicked in. He knew he shouldn't take anything. None of it was his. It belonged to

Al or Augusta. He would worry more about it on the walk to town and sort it all out later. At that moment, he could only pack the boxes and pickle jar back where he had found them, put the board back in place, and head to the clinic in town. And so, he did.

ARSENIC, ASSAYERS & ASSUMPTIONS

The drive back from Pikeview had given Phoebe the time and space to think and relax. She had gotten home after dark and was ready for bed as soon as she walked in the door of the rented trailer. After two long days in a row, a deep sleep was welcomed by her tired mind and body.

When the alarm went off at seven the next morning, she hit the snooze button. Typically, she would lie in bed and think through everything on her current case—what had been looked at, what needed investigating, whom to talk with, and what had been overlooked. That morning was no different.

The trip to Pikeview had been a real eye opener. She had a much better picture of Old Al, or "Albert" as his wife called him. Somehow calling him Albert seemed more befitting considering his age, occupation, and dedication to the tough life of a prospector. It appeared that hunting for gold had worked well for him, and his wife obviously benefited from his efforts. Of course, Queennie always worked hard for a living, but in the end, Al continued to give her money, and she obviously felt entitled to ask for more. Prospecting appeared to be a profitable occupation.

Queennie was initially bitter over her Albert's leaving their life together, but over the years she had adjusted to it. She had her business, her motorcycles, and Albert giving her money—a real life trifecta. Phoebe had noticed that Queennie did not shed a tear with the news of Al's passing. Though a tear almost squeaked out, she remained dry-eyed, seeming genuinely shocked at first, yet shifting quickly into acceptance of his passing.

Then there was the stack of thirty or so coins he had given her. Phoebe thought back to her own surprise at seeing them in Queennie's kitchen. It is illegal to make your own money. Of course, that was a moot point since Al was un-arrestable in his present condition.

Nevertheless, she wondered, *was he making the coins? How did he do it? Gold is too soft to be a coin by itself. Banks don't deal in gold flakes, dust, or otherwise, so he'd need an assayer or some kind of a dealer. What would one of those coins be worth in the market today?*

That was a Bingo moment! Phoebe hadn't thought about the need for an assayer. *Is there an assayer in Oresville? Or close by? There certainly has to be one somewhere in the Arkansas Valley.* Maybe Roz or Carrie Jean could point her in the right direction. She decided she'd call Queennie and ask her how she handled the coins.

Speaking of Carrie Jean, Phoebe had promised her an update for the E-Blast! She certainly did not want to panic the good citizens of Green County with an announcement or headline "Death by Arsenic!" That would be Carrie Jean's style, and it would likely send people into a buying frenzy over bottled water.

Phoebe had still not come to any final conclusions about the single coin under Old Al's body. If he had given Queennie enough coins to do a business deal, maybe he had kept one that he just carried, like a good luck charm or talisman.

Queennie had said that when she rode off early Monday morning, Albert was sitting on an old, worn out camp chair, staring off toward the mountains and absently playing with a coin, flipping it, rolling it over his fingers, a seemingly nervous habit. Sometime between Queennie's leaving and the arrival of Augusta, he died, and the entire area had been swept clean but for a random tire print on a rock, Augusta's footprints, a cigarillo butt, and the gold coin beneath him.

Phoebe took out her phone and searched for the photos she had taken at the scene. The fragments of evidence were finally beginning to make some sense. Old Al must have died where he was sitting, falling off the chair with the coin falling, too, and presto, a Last Hurrah coin was pressed neatly under his body.

I'll have it checked for fingerprints, she thought, *or did I already request that? I was so tired after the first day, I just don't remember. Well, pieces are starting to fit together.*

What was still unsettling for her was the memory of Beautiful Officer Masterson in the driver's seat next to her. She thoroughly enjoyed her time with him in Greenstone. He seemed the strong, silent type. More like just shy. And there was a comment he made about "pretty." What was that about? She hadn't caught it all, as she was too distracted by the mess of scattered papers and bits of clutter strewn about Bart's patrol car, mentally arranging the pieces of her potential homicide case, and getting ready to meet Hank's mother.

Ah, yes, Mrs. Klingfus, her mind sorted. *Talk about clueless. She was a real piece of work.* According to Beautiful Bart, when he had told the woman that he had seen her daughters at the playground and her son, George, at the town's arcade, she went on and on, practically blaming her oldest son for moving out and leaving her to parent her own children.

I could call Bart to see if the kids are in school today, she grinned. *Any excuse to talk with him.*

256

The coffee break she shared with him that morning and the dinner mid-afternoon were so casual, so comfortable, like they had known one another for some time. Certainly, different from the way her morning had begun—passing out at the cop shop was hardly a graceful introduction. As they were leaving the restaurant, he had actually put his hand on Phoebe's back, lightly touching her, as if guiding her out the door. It had been a long time since she felt comfortable with anything like that. Was it the slight tingle she had felt with his touch? Maybe him being in Greenstone and her being there in Oresville was a good thing, but down the road? Phoebe nearly said out loud, *I'll reminisce over this another day.*

First she would rise to greet the day, then meet with Doc Watson to go over the arsenic levels from Hank's blood test. Follow the arsenic . . .

P hoebe walked into the Sheriff's Department at nine o'clock sharp. She heard Roz's typical and often unnecessary, "Good Morning, we're having a great day at the Green County Sheriff's Office. Rosalind Marie Boudreaux speaking."

The night patrol shift had ended, and the morning shift started, but Bill Diamond was probably still over at the county gym working out. Roz had just answered a call and smiled, nodding her head in greeting to Phoebe. Phoebe headed back to the office she shared with others and called Doc.

When Doc answered, they got right down to business. "How'd it go with Al's wife?"

Phoebe filled him in on the trip to Pikeview and the stop at Greenstone. Then it was her turn to get caught up about the arsenic test results.

Doc reported that both Augusta and Hank had higher than acceptable levels of arsenic. Obviously, Hank had been traveling around the mountains, likely drinking whatever Al was drinking, minus Augusta's Special Tea, so that came as no surprise. When they were tested on Tuesday, Doc had asked both of them to come back to the clinic on Thursday for another test. If both of their levels were dropping, that would confirm Doc's theory that the arsenic was from contaminated wells at the Last or the Higgins' cabin. He expected if both of them were drinking fresh, clean city water for two days, their arsenic levels would be dropping.

Doc and Phoebe decided they needed to get water samples from the Last, as well as the cabin where Al spent every winter. Doc volunteered to drive the coroner's truck and invited Phoebe to come along, saying he'd pick her up at her office when he was ready to go.

Phoebe called the cell phone number Queennie had given her, and Queennie answered on the first ring. She sounded more relaxed than the last time they had spoken, and from the sound of the background noise, she was back to work in her shop, Radiators-R-Us.

Phoebe spoke loudly over the racket so as to be sure to be heard, "We received the final results from the autopsy, confirming that Albert did, indeed, die of prolonged arsenic exposure. We will be testing several wells in the mining areas around Oresville to determine where the arsenic is coming from. The town's water department assures us that their mountain stream sources test clean. I thought you'd want to know."

Queennie thanked her for following up and said she wasn't surprised. "Prospecting had its challenges. With Albert, those drawbacks appeared to be life-altering. I always told him to spend some of his money, get a place, and be comfortable for the winter months, but he was too cheap to even consider that. Any of his belongings can be given away, thrown away, or burned, for all I care. The mule included. If you find any money, you know who to call. You've got my number," she chuckled.

Phoebe chose to ignore her sarcasm. She deserved the right to vent after all. "Yesterday when we were in your kitchen, we looked at the coins Albert gave you. I'm curious, what will you do with them?"

"Oh, that's easy," Queennie was still smiling. "I have a longtime friend who's a goldsmith. Really more of an assayer than a goldsmith. Not too many in the gold mining business around Pikeview. Anyway, I just take the coins to her, and she exchanges them for the going rate on gold. I come out with cash. Of course, this is all dependent on the market, so a coin today is not the same value as a coin a year ago. It works for me, and she's a friend."

"Okay, thanks," Phoebe replied, as another piece of the puzzle fell into place. "I was just wondering how it all works. And if I find any coins or gold in his belongings, you'll be the first to know." She went on, "Yesterday when we talked, you asked when Albert's body would be released. It will be released today. Do you have some ideas regarding his last wishes?"

"Nope," Queennie said flatly, "we never talked about that, but he spent most of his adult life up there on the mountain, so I think I'd like to have him cremated, and I'll spread his ashes around the Sunshine, since that's where we always met when I came to see him."

"I think most of this would work, Queennie, but there is a law against the ashes part, so I'd just as soon not hear what you just said about spreading them on National Forest property, okay?"

Queennie grunted in acknowledgement and went on, "You mentioned that Albert occasionally spent time at the Elks Club. I assume he knew a few folks there. Could a memorial service be held there in the next few days, maybe? I'd pay for whatever it would cost. I feel like I owe him that much. There's no other family, just Albert and me. Of course, some of my Pikeview friends might also want to come along for a motorcycle ride through the mountains."

Phoebe explained that the Club manager, Willie Friedrich, would be the person to talk to about making such arrangements. She had no idea what the drill would be for a funeral at an Elks Lodge.

"Alright," she nodded, "I can make a call to Willie and have him contact you, but as next of kin, you'll need to talk with Doc Watson, the coroner who also owns the mortuary, to schedule the cremation."

Queennie said she'd make the call to Doc while waiting for a call from Willie. She would ask if the service could be arranged for the upcoming Saturday. The sooner the better.

Phoebe gave Doc's phone number to Queennie, then hung up and called Willie, leaving him a message with Queennie's number regarding a service for Albert, aka Old Al.

Hearing Bill and Joe in the hallway, she hustled from her desk to bring them both up to speed. Joe spoke first while tugging on his left ear, "Phoebe, I didn't think going to Pikeview yesterday was a good thing to do." He paused for her response. Nothing. "With this said, did you get any information for us?"

Standing at Joe's office doorway, Bill was nodding his head in agreement and ready to add his two cents. Clearing his throat, he chimed in, "I tried to tell her to hold off, Joe, but she'd have none of that."

Phoebe was not about to let either of them criticize her decision. Her case. Her rules.

"As it turns out, my trip to Pikeview was exactly what this case needed. I notified Old Al's next of kin, his wife, Martha. If our timetable is correct as to time of death, she was the last person to see him alive. And paying a visit to the Klingfus family in Greenstone provided plenty of info on the kid's background. You know, the one who tagged along with Old Al all summer? He needs to go back to school and finish up his high school diploma."

"Well," said Joe, ignoring her obvious successes, "I'm not arguing with you, but next time get my permission to use a department vehicle before you run off into another county." He continued tugging at his ear while she continued staring at him blankly with no comment.

Silently, she wondered, *Why only the left ear? Is it bigger than the other one?*

Ignoring the comments from both of them, Phoebe continued the readout on the kid and the wife, minus the part about Beautiful Bart.

"I'll leave it to you two to make a public statement as to the cause of death." As far as Phoebe was concerned, dumping the PR statement on them would give them something to do and satisfy Carrie Jean. She was certain the public statement would become a carefully worded spin job with the help of Carrie Jean's boss, Jesús Garcia.

"Fine. As Sheriff, I'll take it on and maybe stroll over to the bakery. Garcia is probably there. He's just the guy to bring into this one. Bill, care to join me?"

Phoebe shifted her vest. In a twist at their blatant dismissal of her, she watched them walk away and grumbled sarcastically, "Thanks so much for the invite, *not.*"

Bill hustled close behind Joe, while simultaneously checking his own reflection in the window of the office door. Good to go! He was sure there was a double-glazed donut with his name on it, along with an extra-large mug of steaming hot coffee waiting for him just across the street.

"Good Morning, we're having a great day at the Green County Sheriff's Office. Rosalind Marie Boudreaux speaking."

Joe turned and shot *the look* at Roz. The way she answered the department's main line irritated him to no end. Still pulling on his left ear, he stepped out the front door with Bill on his heels, just as Doc Watson entered through the back.

With everyone coming and going and phones ringing off the hook, Phoebe called down the hallway, "Up front here, Doc."

"Yes, Augusta," Roz said into the phone, "she's here, but heading out. Hold on."

Roz nodded her head to Phoebe, "It's Augusta, can you take this?" and handed her the receiver.

Phoebe listened a moment, and replied, "Yes, Augusta. We're headed up there right now to test the well water at your cabin and The Last Hurrah." She listened another minute and responded, "Let me see if there's room for another passenger. Stand by." She reached across Roz to hit the hold button. Doc checked his watch.

After a few short sentences, Doc and Phoebe agreed to have Augusta ride along with them, both having to admit they had only a general idea of the cabin's whereabouts. But "general" could mean hours of riding around on various dead-end mountain trails, for which neither had the time on such a busy day.

Augusta said she would head right over and meet them in the Green County parking lot. Phoebe poured herself a shot to go from the nearly boiled dry coffee pot.

Roz again picked up a phone call on the official line and responded, "Carrie Jean, I think Joe and Bill were headed over to the bakery, but you didn't hear that from me." She hung up the phone, and with a smug look on her face, said, "No reason they can't work and drink coffee at the same time, right?" Phoebe smiled and hustled out the door behind Doc.

Augusta was waiting in the parking lot. Doc motioned them all to his Green County Coroner's truck where Augusta promptly claimed "shotgun" and Phoebe stretched out in the back seat.

They slowly threaded their way along the forest service road in search of the turnoff to the Higgins' cabin. By-passing several side-turns that were obviously well-used, they went on in search of a trail more overgrown and obscured by rocks, weeds, and woods. Though it had been a while since Augusta had been to the cabin, she instinctively knew the route, and they arrived less than an hour later. Doc parked the truck in front, right next to the well pump and announced, "Honey, we're home." They all chuckled.

Phoebe was impressed with the beauty of the location. It was in the middle of a thick stand of aspen trees, which already had the pale green look of early fall. She stood admiring the scenery while Doc pulled his equipment from the truck-bed. Augusta stretched and headed to unlock the cabin door.

Grabbing the pump handle on the well, Doc pushed and pulled patiently until the water flowed freely. He caught a clean sample for the test kit. It would be a wait of twelve minutes for the sample strip to show colors related to arsenic.

While they waited, Doc inspected some old cans of weed killer and insecticide stored under the lean-to. Several of the cans showed contents containing arsenic.

Augusta unlocked the front door and went into the kitchen. Phoebe joined her. Wearing the most genuine smile Phoebe had seen on her face since that fateful Monday morning, Augusta offered to give Phoebe a tour of the entire cabin. One room had a bed. The kitchen looked to be fully furnished. Augusta reminded Phoebe that she let Al stay there during the winter months, as he took care of the building in exchange for free rent. She purposely skipped the part about Al using her great-grandfather's coining equipment.

Doc came in and spotted the hand pump at the kitchen sink. "Augusta," he said, "is this a separate well from the yard pump?"

"I believe so," she answered.

Quickly, Doc pulled out another test kit and took a sample from that second well.

In the stream of dusty light, Phoebe noticed the butt marks on the seat of one chair, and the table looking like someone had taken a swipe across it as if to clean it off.

"Augusta, has someone been here recently?" Phoebe asked. "This table has a spot that looks dusted, like someone was sitting here having a meal or something."

"Yes," Augusta replied, "Hank came over yesterday to be sure the cabin was still standing. It gave him something to do."

Interrupting their riveting conversation, Doc reported the tested water from both wells showed contamination with high levels of arsenic.

"Those test kits work fast," Phoebe noted, "and the results seem to solve the question of where Al got the arsenic."

"Well, no pun intended, that's that," Doc said matter-of-factly. "Let's head over to the Last and see about the well water there."

Augusta locked up the cabin, Doc loaded up the truck, and they headed out. He and Phoebe both advised Augusta to bring in some help and close off both contaminated wells.

"I'll get around to it as soon as I get some extra time," Augusta brushed them off. "No one is ever here, and with Al out of the picture, any lost hiker can take their chances." Spoken like a true, independent mountain woman.

On the drive over to The Last Hurrah, Augusta sat in the back seat of the coroner's truck, reflecting on what Hank had reported to her the day prior, when he came to town for the arsenic test at the clinic. Technically, the gold and coins Hank had told her that he found, belonged to her since they were on her property. Possession is nine-tenths of the law. The quandary was about what to do with the gold. Certainly, the kid was entitled to some kind of pay for his summer labors with Al. Not much, but some.

During the infrequent times he had overindulged in adult beverages or Special Tea, Al had made it a point to let Augusta know that he occasionally gave money to his wife. Actually, regularly. Augusta had no way of knowing the amount he had given to her, but she was clear that he did give her money, and Augusta felt a twinge of jealousy.

Aside from all that, she still wrestled with what to do about the money Al owed the kid. She paid her college hires a flat five hundred a week, which included room and board. She also funded scholarships each year at several engineering schools. Generous, she liked to think. Hank would not be at that pay level, of course, but maybe *two* hundred dollars, cash, no taxes, for each of the eight or nine weeks he had worked. She believed Al would have eventually paid the kid something, were he still alive. Al was frugal, maybe more like cheap, but fair was fair.

Then there was the matter of what to do with the rest of the gold after she paid Hank. In the past, she had always split the coins with Al. Her share for doing absolutely nothing was a solid thirty percent of the summer take. Hank had reported there were many coins and a small pickle jar of gold dust and flakes under the floorboards. She surmised that the stash of dust and flakes must have been the gold Al and Hank had prospected over the summer, waiting to be turned into more coinage over the winter.

Hank had no idea how many coins were there. He reported, ". . . a lot." It must have been Al's retirement savings. Augusta didn't really need those coins for her own personal use. There were a few non-profits in town that could use a windfall. TuTu at the Washateria regularly waived laundry fees and threw in breakfast with a *Mary* for those in need. Certainly, some of Al's coins could help continue her philanthropy. And the Women in Mining her mom helped to start back in the early 1970s, could always use some extra funding. There were lots of possibilities.

The day before, when Augusta had gone to the local post office to spar with the local Postmaster, she had gotten a letter from her mom, Anne Louise. She and Uncle Quinton were moving back from France in time for Thanksgiving. Tired of drinking burgundy wine and eating oysters most days on the Normandy coast in the French fishing village of Port-en-Bessin-Huppain, Anne figured it was time to be with family for the foreseeable future and hang out with people who spoke English, or at least spoke a language she could understand.

Augusta posited she would have Uncle Q melt the gold from the pickle jar and make it into coinage. He had taught Al how to process the gold into coin several years ago, just before he and Anne Louise left for France. Being a retired assayer, Uncle Q could very well cash out the rest of the coins stashed at the Higgins' family cabin. Problem solved.

As they pulled up to The Last Hurrah, Doc asked Augusta if she was napping or just tired of their company.

"Amazing how just slowing down, one can get a better look at the world and life in general," Augusta told him.

Doc gave her a quizzical look in the rearview mirror. Phoebe cocked her head as if to hear more, but silence from Augusta was all that filled the truck's cab.

Augusta had a plan all her own, and she would execute it before winter set in. She was absorbed in thinking about the Old Farmer's Almanac prediction of an early fall with a late spring. Or was it a late fall and an early winter? Well, one or the other.

Not surprisingly, given the toxic nature of mine tailings, Doc's test found arsenic in the water at The Last Hurrah. "You've got to close this well, too, Augusta."

Augusta squinted her eyes, "Yeah, yeah, but right now my priority is to get through the next few days and a memorial service for my friend, Al."

OLD AL'S DAY

The kitchens of Oresville were in high gear Saturday morning. It always happens, as with any death in a small town, that it feels more personal, more real. Even if the person was not a high-profile leader, big contributor, or family presence, as was the case with Al's almost invisible, yet legendary part in the fabric of Oresville.

The expansive sweep of Carrie Jean's E-Blast! on Wednesday announced the cause of Old Al's death, followed on Thursday by an obituary announcing the date and time of his memorial service, with a reminder notice on Friday. The service would bring the townspeople together to not only celebrate Old Al's life, but also to mourn the passing of a fellow member of their community.

Though small in numbers, Oresville was strong in mutual support. Al and Rose were recognized by all. The question of what would happen to Rose was still up in the air. She seemed to be happy on the outskirts of town, grazing in Augusta's rolling front yard. Her tolerant neighbors remained in *pregnant pause* mode.

As Oresville's volunteer event organizer, Roz shifted into high gear to coordinate what was needed to make a memorable memorial gathering. TuTu would conduct the service, since she had once been a minister and currently doubled as a Justice of the Peace and off-the-grid notary. She had a way with words and the gift of compassion. If someone in need of clothes or a meal came into her Washateria, TuTu was right on it. Her care-giving nature applied to Old Al, both then and now.

Carrie Jean and Phoebe would provide the one song for the memorial service. Carrie Jean was locally recognized as having a good, if not quite great, voice. She and Phoebe had been singing together since they were young, and Phoebe added a guitar right after puberty. With Phoebe on guitar, and their intuitive knowledge of one another's musical limitations, they could pretty much cover any misplaced words, varied notes, or off-key squeaks.

Roz had decided the appropriate tune for the occasion would be her Gramma Anne's fav' by Hank Williams: "I'll Never Get Out of This World Alive."

Phoebe and Carrie Jean were ready to go after a hurried practice that morning.

A twelve-noon potluck reception was scheduled to follow the eleven o'clock memorial service. Willie was surprised to learn that Old Al was not an official member of the Club, but had been only an infrequent visitor. Although Willie was always good-natured about the fine print of membership, if the headquarters of the B.P.O.E. were to find out he had allowed an official Elks Departure Ceremony for a non-member, well, there would have been hell to pay. Instead, he and Roz worked out a "Community Fond Farewell," and the entire community was, of course, invited.

Carrie Jean and Roz worked together to be sure attendance would be high. Willie moved the usual three o'clock Saturday Happy Hour pricing to begin at noon. Members only, of course. All others would pay full price. Willie's daughters, Jennifer and Ann, agreed to waitress, and Rose Mary would hostess the affair. Brian would be stationed behind the bar.

Flowers continued arriving all morning on that perfect, late summer, eye-busting blue day. Willie was hands-on in the Club's kitchen, baking an extra-large batch of Chex Mix and an extra-large roaster filled with his homemade baked beans. Well-known for her extemporaneous public speaking skills and total recall of Bible verse, TuTu was scheduled to arrive a full hour ahead of the service.

Brian, looking dapper in a somber black shirt, sleeves rolled to his elbows, and white satin tie knotted neatly at his throat, lined up glasses of water for his two favorite female customers.

Both dressed in mourning black, Phoebe and Carrie Jean were stationed side by side at the bar. Phoebe in her bootcut black jeans, a black Henley, and a black denim jacket over the Henley, sipped her short water while she waited for Augusta to arrive. Her purple Dr. Martens combat boots were only for special events, and that event was very special.

Carrie Jean amply filled out a new pair of black leggings and a black lowcut long-sleeved t-shirt like a ripe tomato ready to burst. A white satin scarf wrapped her neck in a Christmas bow. Phoebe could not help but notice it was the same fabric as Brian's tie. *What's going on here?* she wondered. The past few days had been a flurry of activity and the matching tie thing made her feel a little out of touch with her social circle of friends. Had she missed the memo?

Decked out in a black satin baseball jacket, a v-neck white satin cami, and black sequined pencil skirt, Roz had opened the Club at nine in the morning. Directing the set up for the service, she happily bossed around the wait staff, who did their best to keep up with her free advice. Roz was in her mode of over-thinking each and every detail, but that was what made her events so perfect. Roz put the *P* in *Party*.

Her specialty, potato salad without noticeable eggs, was fresh that morning. Visible eggs were unacceptable. They had to be overprocessed to the nth degree, hard boiled, and then pureed beyond any kind of taste or recognition to be passable. However, in her haste that morning, she had recruited help from a friend, Libby, who had undercooked the potatoes, giving Roz's usually tasty potato salad an unusual crunchy texture. In fact, the salad was closer to a break-a-tooth chewable level. Roz jokingly blamed her friend, Libby, who thought the crunch would be a special touch. Nonetheless, it was tagged an "extra" and the wait staff decided to hold it in the kitchen in case of nuclear attack.

Augusta came into the Club early enough to catch up with the usual crowd at the bar. Brian quickly poured her a Bloody Mary, her usual breakfast of champions. She directed him to start a tab and to add a round of Marys for the standard early attendees. Dressed in honor of her friend, Al, Augusta looked like a cowgirl headed to the stock show. She rocked a buffalo hide skirt that had been hand-beaded with seed beads by native Ute tribal members, a pair of Lucchese Black Tooled Eden cowboy boots that cost more than what Phoebe made in six weeks of salary, and a matching shell tunic that set off a light musical ring as she took delivery of the Mary.

Hearing the ring, August hesitated and looked around the bar. All eyes were on her, and she raised her glass in a toast to Al, her friend and equal in the mining business. *Salute!*

Settled into her spot at the bar, Augusta carefully looked at the two ladies already there. They smiled at her, and all three watched as Roz ran around getting everything ready for the service.

"She's the right person for this party," said Carrie Jean. All three nodded, sipping their Marys.

Phoebe admired her special friends, noticing that Augusta appeared to have a smudge of something dark like charcoal or ashes on her cheek. Maybe she had started lighting her prop cigarettes amid the stress of it all? She kindly handed a tissue to Augusta and gestured to her cheek.

Like well-acquainted friends, the three ladies started to catch up on their lost time from several weeks back when Augusta had last been to town. Al's passing was an unavoidable topic.

"Had he listened to the age-old caution to 'never drink fresh-looking water in the mountains nor yellow snow in town,' he might still be alive and roaming the mountains today," someone said. It was clear the character he brought to their community would be noticeably absent.

Everyone rationalized that at Old Al's old age, passing as he did was a blessing. "No one wants to linger. When it's your time, it's your time," was another comment overheard from farther down the bar.

"You'll never get out of this world alive," Carrie Jean hummed the song's best line.

Phoebe laughed out loud, and they ordered up another round.

Augusta took interest in the talk at the bar regarding the weather, early fall or late fall, and winter coming. Brian overheard the conversation and pulled out his dog-eared, ragged, overused Old Farmer's Almanac. He kept a copy behind the bar for just those kinds of pressing questions. In spite of the occasion, the Club was feeling almost normal.

Augusta had talked to Hank the day before at the clinic while they were both getting their blood re-checked for arsenic levels. Their levels were coming down nicely, Augusta told everyone that she would be getting a new well drilled the next spring at the Last. She had given Hank $1,200 as payment for his summer labors with Al. She tried to get in some last words of encouragement with Hank, and made him promise that he would finish high school. Not one word was exchanged regarding the coins and gold he had found at the Higgins' family cabin.

Having never been to a funeral or memorial service, Hank had planned to be at the Club at eleven o'clock sharp, eat lunch, accept any leftovers to take for the long drive back to Greenstone, and head out. He had used Augusta's cell phone to call home. His mom and dad were happy to hear he would be returning, ending his Early Gap Year. The bad news was that his old bedroom had become the family office and the parents' retreat. He would have to sleep on the couch, but only for a few months until some arrangements could be made or until he graduated, whichever came first.

Arriving at the service on the early side of eleven, he was looking sharp and uncomfortable in a new shirt, shorts, and flip flops all purchased at the local dollar store. Augusta assumed the windfall of money was likely burning a hole in his pocket. Just as the ladies were being kind and ordering up a pop with peanuts on the side for him, the noise of motorcycles arriving interrupted their conversation.

It was the kind of day that was ideal for a motorcycle ride. Queennie and her friends, all similarly dressed in designer jeans, custom-made leather chaps and matching jackets, parked their Harleys side by side. The townsfolk were arriving as Queennie came into the Club. She stood motionless taking in the attendance, the Club, the potluck, and was visibly moved to see such a large gathering for her dearly departed husband.

Rose Mary welcomed Queennie and her friends, helping them pick a place down front for special seating. Roz killed the zydeco music she had playing low in the background, freshened her Death Red lipstick, and straightened her cami, thinking, *Ready for action.*

Augusta leaped off her bar stool and headed over to greet Doc, who was looking around for a place to sit. Carrie Jean was still humming the upcoming tune as a bit of rehearsal and looking at Brian, who smiled, "Sounds good."

As they all migrated to the meeting room for the service, the phone rang. Brian answered, "We're having a Memorial Service at 10-5."

He listened for a minute. Nodding at Phoebe, he handed the phone to her. The dispatcher was calling for Phoebe, on call as the emergency backup for the Sheriff's Department that weekend. A report had come in that Augusta's family cabin was on fire, and the county volunteer firefighters were responding. Color draining from her face, Phoebe looked directly at Augusta who cracked a slight smile.

THE END THE END THE END THE END THE END
THE END THE END THE END THE END
THE END

Or is it . . .?

ACKNOWLEDGMENTS

First and foremost, we want to extend our appreciation to the local law enforcement men and women of Chaffee, Lake, and Weld counties in Colorado, and Pima county in Arizona, whose flexibility and diligence with the citizens in their areas make livin' large in these areas comfortable, interesting, and safe

We must thank our families who have supported our laborious writing, and reviewing, and laughing at the littlest bit of nonsense. Our husbands and our children's undying, loving support and patience helped us keep our heads on straight, pulled us back from the ledge as needed, and vetted our focus on Phoebe's adventures in life and law enforcement. We love you.

Also, we want to publicly acknowledge Deb Cornell and Becky Sloboda for their early on editorial insights, praise, and encouragement that gave us the strength to continue and the vision to grow this story. To all of you who have graciously allowed us to use and grow from your experiences, it's all about the stories we accumulate as we grow. A heartfelt virtual hug going out to Dennis Butler for his creative chapter name, Mary Henson for her friendship and love of Sazerac, Nancy Taylor for her expertise in designing clipart, DeDe Williams for her historical recollection of the area, and Jon Nilsestuen for his wonderful photography. A High-5 going out to Felix Whitticase, who christened Carolyn Gary, with the byline, "She puts the P in Party!" And she does!

We extend our thanks to our friend and Pima County, Arizona, Senior Forensic Technician, Wendy Simms. Our sincere appreciation to her department for allowing us to picture her with their vehicle as the prototype of our gal, Phoebe.

The National Mining and Hall of Fame Museum in Leadville, Colorado, gave us the inspiration for this story. Their collections feature the brave women and men who helped make mining the backbone of growth in Colorado in the 1800s. Our story is included with a collection of short stories in *Mysteries from the Museum* sold in their gift shop at www.MiningHallofFame.org

ACKNOWLEDGMENTS

Additionally, we salute the leadership and expertise of fellow author Jennifer Sweete (JenniferSweete.com). As President of the Chaffee County Writers Exchange (CCWritersExchange.org) she brings together people from varying backgrounds and writing experiences to share their skills and help one another grow. Her editing is supportive, corrective, creative, and patient at all levels, and her contribution to the cover design much appreciated. Her knowledgeable assistance with the process of self-publishing and marketing has also been invaluable. Thanks, Jen, what a ride, eh?

How can you help us? We want to continue to explore the world of women in law enforcement today and those of us who reside in small towns. Please share your experiences with us! Every little bit helps us and encourages us to expand the adventures of Phoebe and friends and the Sheriff Department of Oresville, Colorado.

Please tell your friends, family and the world about this book! Write a review about *The Last Hurrah, A Phoebe Korneal Mystery* on Amazon.com. Visit us on our website at BnGbooks.com and share your feedback at PhoebeKoeneal@gmail.com.

READING GROUP

1. What do you think are the challenges for women in law enforcement today? In the story, Phoebe moves from a big city in another state to a small mountain town in order to further her career. Can we speculate about the personal opportunities in a small town vs. a big city, especially in law enforcement? What are the trade-offs, pros and cons?

2. Is there a difference in law enforcement in small towns versus large cities? In one example, Phoebe is jaywalking from the County building to the Club. Do we think it is easier to get away with breaking the law in small towns or big cities? What does this say about Phoebe and her personal standards? Can we cite other examples of her personal standards in the story?

3. How do women relate to Old Al's wife, Martha AKA Queennie, in her non-traditional job and her lifestyle? What do we think when we see a woman owning a radiator shop or riding a Harley? What are the differences between women in nontraditional work in Corporate America vs. other settings? Can we call out the examples as proof one way or the other—easier or not? What are your first thoughts regarding a woman who works on radiators in a shop vs. a woman who owns the shop?

4. There are several women in this story. How do they support each other emotionally? And what are their differences? Can we give examples of how they support one another? What would you expect to see—small community, high altitude, newcomers about the same age? How does Augusta fit in with these newcomers, and how does her age make a difference?

5. Will Phoebe enter into a relationship with Beautiful Man in Greenstone? What examples from the story would make building a relationship with Beautiful Man a challenge to develop? Or examples that could make it easier. Will distance help or hinder?

6. How is the Elks Club important to the culture of Oresville? What are examples from the story of how the Club "works" for Oresville? Cite examples of how Willie runs the Club, and does the example support the community or is it detrimental to the community or the members?

7. What do you think of Old Al and his choices in life? In the story, Old Al left Martha after a few months of marriage. Why, do you think? Did he not want to be married? From the story, what makes you think this way? What does the story say about Al giving money to Martha and why? Was this the right thing to do? Did he owe her money? Do you think he still loved her, even though he left her?

8. Augusta's family history is steeped in the tradition of mining. Why do you think Augusta has chosen the life of a miner rather than the citified life of a wealthy woman? In the story, what are the examples of her choices? Should she give all or some of the coins to Hank? Or to Martha? Why or why not? Is this choice "in character" for her?

9. Hank, at his young age, has made some major life choices. What do you think of his choice to take an *early gap year*? Where were his parents in his decision, and do you agree with his parents' actions? Did he learn anything from the summer? Should he return to high school and complete his education with a diploma or can he make a go of it in Oresville?

There are several characters in this fiction work. Who would you like to see more of in the next book? Please let us know at phoebekorneal@gmail.com. We would love to hear from you! We appreciate your opinions, and are happy to answer your questions and your pleas for more!

Books by

GaGa Gabardi and Judilee Butler

A PHOEBE KORNEAL MYSTERY SERIES

BOOK 3

COMING

SOON!

ABOUT THE AUTHORS

We stumbled into our collaboration beginning with a short story project *Mysteries From the Museum* for the National Mining Hall of Fame and Museum in Leadville, Colorado. From there, we decided *why not take the next step and develop characters, storyline, and a setting all within the context of our joint sense of humor?*

Using technology to jump the hurdles of our distant locations—2,000 miles between our homes—we were able to develop our character, Phoebe Korneal (pronounced Cor-nell) and grow a framework around a small mountain town, using Colorado history for background.

As we were putting the finishing touches on our story, the Pandemic hit! Lucky for us, it was time for editing and the safety measure of confinement became a triple opportunity to focus, rewrite, and laugh together.

We hope that you can sit back and enjoy the ride that *The Last Hurrah* is intended to be and, at the finish, be wanting to read our next adventure!

Meantime, we invite you to share questions, comments, and extraneous outbursts at our website BnGbooks.com and by email at PhoebeKorneal@gmail.com.

GAGA GABARDI

Graduating from college, my one thought was to leave Minnesota and live where the weather is phenomenal, but I never made it to southern California!

I retired from a career in telecom with a Master's in Project Management, another in Business, and an Advanced Project Degree from Stanford (thank you, corporate world). Completing my private pilot license, I needed money for 'av' fuel ... back to work—this time consulting, teaching, course development, a welcome change alongside the birth of my first grandson who named me GaGa. Thank you, B.

Writing with Judilee was a way I could add levity within the confines of the pandemic, reach out to others to share our mutual experiences, and fine-tune my storytelling.

Hubby and I live in the Colorado mountains. It's an easy pace for us with enough space to enjoy camping, fishing, and riding the rough mountain trails. I can't make up these experiences!

ABOUT THE AUTHORS

I hope you enjoy *The Last Hurrah,* get a chuckle here and there, learn a bit regarding Colorado history, and at the end, wonder what happens next.

JUDILEE BUTLER

Born and raised in New York, I attended the State University of New York at Brockport and taught Kindergarten for several years. Settling in North Carolina, I completed a Master's Degree in Special Education. At that point, the corporate world was calling and I began my career with IBM.

Twenty years later, with the family safely launched into life, my husband and I retired to the central mountains of Colorado. We enjoy a yearly trek to Florida and other parts of the East coast.

Writing with the Chaffee County Writers Exchange opened a whole new world for me. GaGa and I collaborated to write a mystery short story as a fundraiser for the Leadville Mining Museum. We enjoyed creating that so much, we decided to try a cozy mystery series.

Oresville is a small mining town in the high mountains of Colorado. Lots of history, characters, and puzzles for our gal, Phoebe, to solve. The rest is history, as the saying goes.

I hope you enjoy our stories as much as we enjoy writing them.

GAGA AND JUDILEE are available for lectures and select readings. To inquire about a possible appearance, please contact them at phoebekorneal@gmail.com.

They favor locations such as Colorado, Florida, Minnesota, North Carolina, Arizona and Hong Kong. Inquire soon, scheduling time is of the essence.

phoebekorneal@gmail.com

BnGBooks.com

Made in the USA
Columbia, SC
05 January 2022

53569406R00173